JUDE

N GRAY

BOOKS

By N Gray

The Dana Mulder Suspense Thriller Series

Deadly Pattern

Devil Mountain

Chasing Evil

Nightcrawler

Horror

What's for Dinner

Creature Features

Monster Features

Thrillers

Lady Killer

More from N Gray

writing as Natalie Michaels

Steve Campbell Psychological Suspense Thrillers

The Last Girl

The Bone Forest

The White Dahlia

I See You

Death in the City

More from N Gray

writing as SD Syns

The Diaries

Red Lace Diaries

www.ngraybooks.com

Vinci Books

vinci-books.com

Published by Vinci Books Ltd in 2026

1

A CIP catalogue record for this book is available from the British Library.
Paperback ISBN: 9781036702274
The EU GPSR authorised representative is Logos Europe, 9 rue Nicolas
Poussion, 17000 La Rochelle, France contact@logoseurope.eu

Chapter One

Flynn and Penn vanished that one snowy day a week ago. When we searched for them, their scent and tracks had disappeared; like they never existed.

Their disappearance didn't sit well with me, along with other parts of that day felt off. It snowed when it shouldn't have. The air was stuffy during the search in the forest, along with a constant buzz of power in the atmosphere.

Being an amateur sleuth-tiger-shifter, I needed to investigate the events more closely; whenever I entered the forest near where they disappeared, I still felt the pull of that power lingering in the air. This told me that something was still there, something was keeping the power alive.

Flynn and Penn were gone for five days, only to reappear with an intriguing story to tell. The events that took place over those five days sounded horrible and filled with sinister activities.

A deranged shaman held the two captive, and he almost succeeded in keeping them as hostages in a phantom village deep within the forest in Sterling Meadow.

We were all elated they were home and unharmed, but I couldn't help shake the feeling that something else had happened. It wasn't only the shaman's power that kept the people in their ghostly village, but something otherworldly.

Something else was out there, and I would figure it out.

"I really wish you would leave it be," Flynn said, munching on a slice of toast with a thick layer of blueberry jam. He licked the corners of his mouth but missed a crumb.

"I won't be long," I said, packing a bag of nuts, the sandwich I'd made, and two liters of water into a backpack.

"Do you have your cellphone?"

"I'm not forgetful like you," I grinned, patting my jacket chest pocket where I kept my cellphone. If only Flynn had his cellphone on his person that day, we could've rescued them in time.

"Ha, you're funny," Flynn smiled; ever since he and Penn's near-death experience, they grew closer every day, and he smiled often. It almost made me smile… Almost.

"I should be back by nightfall," I said, opening the back door to the warehouse we guarded for Léon, our Master Vampire boss. "And if I'm not home, phone me. I might have fallen somewhere and need rescuing." I slapped Flynn's chest, and he almost dropped his toast.

"Don't say that," he grumbled as I closed the back door.

Chapter Two

I traversed the same path Flynn and Penn had walked that fateful day. The hairs on my arms stood up as drops of sweat slipped down my spine.

The potent power continued pulsing in the forest.

I stepped off the path and headed for an old fallen tree. Its bark was rotten with insects crawling in and around it. In the distance, I heard the trickle of a stream.

Here, I felt the cool wind against my damp clothing and felt the sun warm my face and neck. There was no power here. I glanced over my shoulder, focusing on the trees, leaves, and bushes near the path.

Time passed. The wind stopped blowing and the call of the birds silenced.

The leaves moved gently, as if invisible hands were slowly caressing them. The dark green bushes barely moved, but here, too, I caught glimpses of invisible movement; as if someone had walked past.

My thoughts drifted to a cemetery filled with damned souls unable to move freely or where they're meant to be.

Up ahead, the face of the mountain stood ominously, with deep shadows and dark crevices. The sun shone brightly behind the mountain, slowly brightening the rocks and forest floor before me.

I glanced at the worn path once more, and a shudder ran through me. Something was off. This wasn't the forest I'd frequently hiked to enjoy forest bathing; a self-prescribed therapy. No, this forest had changed.

The world moved quickly. Humans worked harder these days and for much longer hours. While their children barely had time to play as kids, and instead became addicted to whichever device was their favorite.

My job fighting evil supernaturals would take its toll on me. So, to quieten my sensitive soul, I'd come here and sit in the calm atmosphere of the trees, leaves, and mountainous shadow to ground myself. To forest bathe.

I sucked in air over my teeth, but sensed nothing out of the ordinary, and approached the path. Once I reached the path the ghostly fingertips of its power touched me as I moved through an invisible film-like bubble.

I stood on the path, closed my eyes, and inhaled deeply. Again, there was nothing different; I smelled damp sand at my feet, the fresh blossoms on a nearby tree, and heard the buzzing of bees. The wind whistled through the tree branches, but there were no other sounds.

As I exhaled, the air popped and my eyes shot open, and I focused ahead of me. Near one of the older oak trees was a sparkly black dot. I cocked my head to the side, waiting, watching, but nothing else happened; it just sparkled. I stepped closer and poked the dot with my index finger. It pulsed and grew rounder.

The sparks of the moving black circle spat at me, reminding me of fireworks that struggled to ignite. I poked it again. It exploded into a firework display and the circle became large enough for me to step through.

When I glanced over my shoulder at the path I'd taken, and then up ahead; I was the only one here. I reached for my cellphone, dialed Flynn's number and he answered on the first ring.

"What's wrong?" He breathed into my ear as if he was running.

"I found something," I said, taking a picture of the large portal, the fireworks surrounding it now only a tiny spark, and sent the picture to Flynn.

"What in the hell is that?" Flynn said. "Don't go in there, Jude. You don't know where that doorway leads."

"I have to go," I said as I reached for the magical gateway. "What if it doesn't open again?"

"Don't gamble with your life, dude. If you go now, you won't be able to return. Come home and we'll all accompany you."

I knew he was wrong. There was a reason the gateway opened for me. If I left now, I doubted it would open again. I only had one chance to see who was behind the portal.

"I'll try to be back by sunset." I ended the call when Flynn's colorful language rose in volume.

I pocketed my cellphone, pulled tightly on my backpack, and entered the portal.

Chapter Three

The boys back at the warehouse would think I was insane doing this but something called to me, and I knew it was something I had to do. I was meant to be in the forest at that moment, and it felt right doing this.

I held my breath as I entered the portal. The step from the forest to the unknown was quick and painless. The air in the portal was sweet and sticky; reminding me of a candy shop. When I opened my eyes, my breath caught in my throat.

The pastel pink sun hung in the sky like a little girl's bedside lamp. The soft pink glow of the sun splashed across the sky and ground, covering it with soft sparkles.

I blinked a few times to make sure I saw correctly. When the new world came into focus, a thin smile tugged on my lips. This world was just as mystical as the fae world.

I slowly took in my surroundings. In the distance stood pyramids of various sizes; The Great Sphinx like the one in Giza but with its nose still attached.

On either side of me stood weeping willows with tiny

faeries fluttering around it, their wings glowed with a gentle light. They were ridiculously cute, making me wish I had a little girl I could show this world to.

Beyond the willow trees were streams that, unlike in the normal world, they flowed in the air with droplets falling to the sand. Here, water seemed to defy gravity.

A bell tolled up ahead, catching my attention. I was about to head that way when the ground beneath my shoes shook and grumbled. Something behind me thumped loudly, as if the person had heavy footsteps when they ran.

The willow tree branches swayed from the shaking ground, and the tiny faeries flew away. I stepped closer to the one willow and blended in with the shadows, but before I could get comfortable, the weeping willow uprooted itself and walked away in search of safety.

I flinched when an enormous foot crashed in front of me, then stepped forward. The giant walked in the sound's direction; the continuous bell ringing would usually annoy me, but not this sound. This soothing chime was pleasant, and I wanted to see more.

I sprinted after the giant to the top of a hill, and stared down at the bustling town. My eyes bounced across the various buildings and at the people living there... people I'd never seen before... supernaturals I'd only heard of.

Blue wolves hurried from one house to the next. Blue female wolves fixed their elegant dresses or skirts as they headed toward the town square, and the male blue wolves wore suits and top hats from the Victorian era. One male even used a walking stick with a silver handle.

I couldn't wrap my mind around the fact that blue were-wolves dressed in such elegant clothing. I was used to Shawn's were-wolves who wore normal twenty-first century clothing. They shredded their clothing when they changed into their wolves at the pull of the full moon, and would walk around like that; all furry.

These alluring blue wolves were strange, yet I couldn't tear my eyes away. Some ladies' dresses were maroon with black sequence over it, while others were a deep purple or emerald green. While some women wore culottes that flared like a dress as they walked. These wolves were progressive considering their attire.

The giant I'd been following sat on the far outskirts of the town with a deep sigh that blew my hair back; literally. Once he was comfortable, he watched the blue wolves with his one blue eye that was positioned in the middle of his forehead. He had no nose or mouth and I wondered how he breathed. The answer to my question came in short bursts of his gills opening and closing on the sides of his neck.

I swallowed hard and stepped backward.

Nothing made sense in this world with its upside-down streams, large giant, and blue wolves. I glanced up at the full moon shining at the same time as the sun. It didn't look like either moved from their spot in the pastel pink sky. This place was as strange as a trippy dream I needed to wake up from.

When icy fingers curled around my upper arm, I froze. I didn't know what creature had grabbed me or what their plans were. But it angered me that I hadn't heard them. Then they spoke.

"Don't worry, Jude," said the sweetest voice I'd ever heard. "We won't hurt you."

As if her saying my name was an invitation, I slowly turned my head and looked directly into the eyes of the voice's owner. Her features were childlike, yet I knew she was a woman with her barely there clothing that covered only her delicate parts.

My body stiffened along with my cock, and I fought the urge to move my dick around in my pants. Oh, to touch her would be an exciting delight; a caress of her soft skin, a kiss here and a lick there. Images of her nakedness flooded my mind and I wanted nothing more than to kiss her.

Her smile reached her eyes, lighting her face, which made her even more beautiful. Her light blue eyes held dark secrets, though the nervousness in them made me cautious of her. Those images I had of her were quickly squashed once I realized that someone so stunningly deadly came with *terms and conditions* better left alone.

"Empress," said a male voice behind her. "I must object to this meeting. It is unnecessary to call everyone here," said the man. He stopped beside her and froze when he noticed me. Tiny blue sparks shot from his fingers to the strands of black hair with light blue streaks as he tucked the strand behind his pointy ears. His pretty lavender-colored eyes strained on mine, and he pursed his lips.

"I'm aware of your view, Olson. This isn't something any wolf can do. I need a powerful tiger," the Empress said, staring at me. It was as if she was the one who had summoned me because she needed me. She needed my tiger.

"And he," Olson said, pointing his bony finger at me. Blue sparks shot from the tip of his index finger, narrowly missing me. "Is the one to help you? Why? Just look at him."

The empress smiled again. There was something magical about her, but, as attractive as she was, I couldn't trust her or anyone from this strange world.

"Yes, Jude will succeed." She winked and squeezed my bicep. "Now, Olson, please go down there and tell everyone

I need five males and five females who will accompany Jude on his quest—"

"Now hold up, your highness. How can I help if I don't know what you want?" I said, raising both palms and stepping out of her grasp. I had to put distance between myself and them.

"In time, Jude. But first, let's drink and get to know one another," the Empress said. Her voice was smooth against my skin, as if she herself was caressing me with her fingertips.

I shuddered and stepped farther back. Her grin widened.

Chapter Four

I glanced out of the window, and that one eye continued glaring at me. Although I didn't know the giant, it looked like he was silently killing me in his thoughts. He continued grumbling outside of the tavern like continuous rolling thunder even though he had no mouth.

I ignored the massive brute, exhaled an annoyed breath, and turned my attention on the table instead. On my right-hand side were five females and on my left were the five males who would join me on my quest. A quest I know nothing about.

When I first saw the town and the blue wolves heading toward the town square, they were all in their wolf form; dark blue fur beneath lavish clothing. Now, they sat before me in their human form. They, like Olson, had pointy ears, lavender-colored eyes, and black hair with blue streaks; except for one female, she had light brown hair. They all looked similar, with slight differences in the shape of the faces and body type.

They were a special breed. If I had to guess what they were, they were clones made from various DNA that included human, fae, were-wolves, and a blue creature. I couldn't fathom their origins—possibly alien.

I was yet to discover what exactly my quest was. For now, everybody ate and drank like it was the last supper and, gods forbid, I was their holy leader about to drag them to hell.

Something popped, and I glared down at the noisy meal; blinking eyeballs, hairy ears, and a bubbling slimy mixture. I pushed the bowl farther away from me, and squeezed the handle of my drink, which tasted like piss. Not that I knew what urine tasted like, but the smell alone convinced me not to drink their local ale.

"Don't you eat meat?" I asked the male closest to me.

The room fell silent, and everyone at the table stared at me. Their death-stare felt like an ice-cold bucket of water drenched over me, yet warm sweat clung to my clothing.

"They are not like the wolves you're used to, Jude," said the Empress. She sat on the opposite end of the table, like we were a couple enjoying dinner with our ten blue and furry children.

"Can you just tell me what's going on?" I asked, rubbing my eyes, then rested my elbows on the table.

Someone on my right gasped, and I sat up.

The Empress sat straight and glowered at me. Her childlike features were now sharp as sinister shadows played on her face. Her light blue colored eyes were now a startling red.

I raised both hands in surrender.

The Empress stood and sauntered toward me.

The males on my left scooted down the table, giving the Empress a place to sit beside me.

"Jude," she said in a condescending tone, and sat down. She crossed her right leg over her left and leaned her elbow on the table. "I need you to retrieve something for me." She glanced up and near her right shoulder was a memory floating in the air like a movie.

I frowned at the strange sight, yet fully engrossed in the vision on display for all to see. Her memory revealed much; she was a queen in Egypt a long time ago, but the man she loved had betrayed her.

As if carried by the wind, someone whispered his name, Firoze; it sounded dreamlike as her memory continued playing.

Firoze buried her alive in a tomb made for them and disappeared with her jewels. Her prized jewel was an amulet that protected her soul and would provide a safe journey into the afterlife.

But she could not enter the afterlife because he had taken her Heart Scarab amulet. To keep herself from spiraling into chaos and destroying her world, she created this world where those who didn't belong anywhere could roam safely and freely.

The Empress would remain in her world until the right person came along worthy enough to retrieve her Heart Scarab amulet.

In her memory-vision, the blue wolves had discovered her world by using the same portal I'd used. They had told her how the evil Shannon had created them; the mad scientist who created his own army, along with his own children using his sperm and that of women who he later killed.

My heart ached for the blue wolves; some of them were born human and then created, while others were born to a human mother and turned into a blue wolf but later died during childbirth.

The scenes in her memory-vision were horrific. When I glanced at the various faces staring at me, I couldn't help but want to help them. Not only the Empress, but everyone seated here.

"The blue wolves may leave whenever they want, but they choose to remain here with me," the Empress said, giving each wolf her attention.

"When they wandered around Sterling Meadow after they killed their creator," the Empress continued. "They became enslaved by the owner of a Shifter Retreat Center and when a major fight broke out, they escaped. It's been devastating for them as much as my situation," she said with a somber expression.

"If you help me, I can maintain this world for myself and the wolves. And with their help," — she pointed at the wolves at my table, — "you and that mighty tiger will defeat him."

How could I not help her and the blue wolves? It was in my nature to help those in need. I was born a were-tiger and my clan guided me through everything. I could only imagine what these wolves had gone through, knowing someone so evil had created them.

I was aware of Shannon's evil activities. It relieved everybody once we destroyed him, and now the aftereffects of his evil doings continued till today. I wondered what else he had created and was hiding from the world.

Olson cleared his throat, and the Empress turned in his direction.

"Mum," Olson continued, clearing his throat again.

"Yes, yes," she waved him away. "I'm sure Jude won't mind if you accompany them."

The lines between Olson's eyes deepened, and he

pursed his lips. He sat down with a huff and folded his arms across his chest.

I wasn't sure what was going on between them, but whatever it was, I hoped Olson wouldn't take it out on me.

Chapter Five

"Are we going into battle?" I asked Jeremy, the only blue wolf blacksmith in this magical town.

"What did the Empress tell you about the man you seek?" Jeremy asked, his blue mustache lifting one side when he pulled a face that told me he was confused.

"Not much, that she needs me to retrieve her Heart Scarab amulet," I said, the lines between my eyes deepening.

Jeremy placed his large sledgehammer on the anvil and gave me his full attention. "The Empress has described Firoze as one of the most dangerous—"

"The Empress said nothing about him being dangerous." I'd witnessed Firoze murder the Empress based on her memory-vision. But I didn't know what really transpired between them, nor did I know what kind of man Firoze was and if he'd killed before.

"When we first arrived in this world, she painted a different picture, Mr. Jude," Jeremy said, shrugging nonchalantly and picked up his sledgehammer again.

I didn't like this. I was going into a battle blind, and it wasn't my fight.

"Perhaps she said nothing because she thinks you are powerful enough to disarm him. You must be a natural-born were-tiger?" He asked, and I nodded. "Well, you are his weakness."

"How?" I asked, frowning. "What do you mean?"

"You'll render him powerless by being in his presence. But, in order to get to him, you'll need this," he said, handing me a gigantic sword, dagger, and a scabbard. "He has an army protecting his pyramid."

"Is he in this world?"

Jeremy shook his head. "No, yours," — he poked a fat finger into my chest, — "but Olson will get you there before you can say *Abracadabra*." Jeremy smiled and his mustache looked like a hairy caterpillar on his upper lip.

I smiled at the strange man but was secretly worried about my so-called quest. I was going into battle with someone who could kill me with a flick of his wrist.

I strapped the scabbard to my waist and slid the sword in. The action was smooth, the way the blacksmith had made them. Then I slipped the dagger into the sheath on my right-hand side.

I rarely fought with a sword. The last time I used one was when I fought Kai at practice. I had knocked him on his ass and stopped before slicing off his head. I was sure I could defend myself against Firoze.

A commotion erupted behind me. I turned around in time to see Olson and the others morph into their blue wolves.

I was a natural born were-tiger, and my shift was painful sometimes. For some shifters there was pain involved; our muscles tore, bones broke, and everything readjusted. But not them; Olson's change was sudden, and it didn't seem like it affected him or the others. I'd never seen a shift happen so peacefully and quickly.

The eleven blue wolves marched in unison, sporting matching battle clothing. It amazed me they all shifted into their blue wolves without shredding their clothing. Like a flick of a light switch, they changed, like it happened easily every day.

I swallowed hard at the sudden change in the atmosphere; the air was thick with that same sweet smell. The sky darkened, painting the town landscape in a dark blue hue. The pretty pink I'd become accustomed to was gone in a blink of an eye.

When a hand grabbed my shoulder, I flinched, grabbed their hand and spun around, readying to break their hand and possibly bite whoever touched me.

"Easy, tiger," the Empress said with humor in her tone. "I'm glad Jeremy has fitted you with your custom-made sword. I had it charmed just right to protect you. Always keep it on your person and don't allow anyone else to touch it. The dagger included." She patted my shoulder. "Promise me one thing, you must kill Firoze with it?"

"Sure," I mumbled.

"Good," she said with a delightful smile and approached the oncoming blue army.

The Empress raised her hands, and the wolves halted.

Now that I could see all of her, she'd changed into something more appropriate for a princess going into battle instead of a striptease. She wore dark makeup around her light blue eyes, making her appear serious and deadly.

A hissing sound caught my attention and, on the floor, slid two snakes, each with two heads. They slithered up the Empress's boots, her thighs, and all the way until they reached her wrists, where they wound their thin bodies around her arms. They stiffened into bracelets as if magic commanded them.

I stepped backward in case something bigger neared us, perhaps attaching itself to her waist, but nothing else moved on the ground that I could see.

"My wolves, I have been waiting for the pink sun's eclipse." The Empress pointed at the dark moon above. The pink sun now blending into the background as the blue moon moved in front of it.

"When night meets day," — the Empress continued, — "the curse my once beloved had cast over me shall be lifted, and I will once again be the rightful owner of my Heart Scarab amulet."

The Empress walked through the sea of blue wolves, turned around and walked back, making sure she touched each wolf.

"Let my touch protect you on your quest." She stopped beside Olson and hugged him. "Take care of my wolves, Olson, and do whatever it takes to bring them all back safely." Then she turned toward me and reached for my hand. "Allow Olson to guide you. He knows more than he lets on, so trust him." She winked.

My eyes flitted to Olson. He stood straighter and raised his head; clearly, he felt good by her praise. When he looked at me, I nodded once in approval. He smiled.

One thing I'd learned from going into battle with shifters I didn't know was to allow them to think we were friends, and I was on their side. The last thing I wanted was fighting among the people meant to protect me.

"As you know, Shannon created Olson and the blue wolves," the Empress continued. "He spliced their DNA with fae, which offered them additional powers. But Olson is the most powerful among them and will provide safe passage to Egypt where you will find my amulet." The Empress squeezed my hand and let go.

"Right, get your weapons," Olson barked, and the ten wolves scattered to collect their items from Jeremy.

While they were busy, the Empress leaned into me and whispered, "Give Olson the satisfaction of being in charge. But it is only you who can retrieve the amulet." She squeezed my biceps, and I could've sworn she purred.

"Do you want to tell me anything else?" I asked, my words were sharp. She didn't tell me everything about Firoze and I was angry. I was about to risk my life for people I'd just met, and they weren't forthcoming about how dangerous Firoze really was.

"But Jeremy already told you the most important part." The Empress' eyes flitted from my eyes to my mouth.

"Sure, but why didn't you?" I pulled my arm out of her grasp and stepped away from her. Once I created distance, the air wasn't as thick and sweet.

Her features morphed into something I could only describe as unpleasant. "I don't see the issue, Jude. You will render him powerless. He is allergic to were-tigers—"

"Which tells me he will do everything in his power to have me killed before I can even get ten feet near him." I crossed my arms over my chest and frowned. I wasn't pleased about this. The Empress seemed unaware that I was risking my life for her.

"What do I receive for helping you? Not once did you ask me to do this for you. You just assumed I'd do it."

The Empress exhaled and glanced down. When she looked up again, her childlike features were back. I hated when she did this. It was as if she had different personalities in that pretty head of hers.

"Please forgive me, Jude." She shook her head. "I did not realize… It's been so long—"

"How long have you been here?"

"Ten years."

"Why haven't you found a were-tiger before now?"

"There were many were-tigers who could help me, but I had to wait for the eclipse that only happens once every ten years. And you were the closest were-tiger I could find at such short notice. It was this day ten years ago when Firoze cursed me and stole my amulet."

"How powerful is he really? And don't lie to me."

"He is a powerful King, but extremely vain. I know in my gut that you have it in you to defeat him." She continued rubbing my arm as if it was a comfort. It was not. Then there was the sweet candy floss smell assaulting my nose.

"His army is weak," she said. "They can't fight the blue wolves, and if my sources are correct, his army has aged or has already died."

"I hope you are right, Empress. And when I return. What do I get out of it?" I asked again.

"When I have my amulet, I will give you anything you want." She smiled sweetly, and I couldn't help it. I still wanted to help her.

Chapter Six

Olson took charge, telling everyone what to do, how to do it, and when. He impressed me; at our first interaction, he seemed uptight and slightly annoying. But the more I got to know him, the more I understood his motives; he genuinely wanted to help his wolves and the Empress. And I suspected he may even love for her, but this was one-sided.

The kind of betrayal the Empress had experienced made me doubt if she could love any man ever again. I couldn't blame her. I'd feel the same if it happened to me.

Once everyone was ready and waiting, Olson channeled his inner magic and conjured a portal, much like the one I'd found in the forest and stepped through to reveal their pink, magical world.

The black hole sparked along its border as it grew larger. When the portal was large enough to walk through, Olsen stepped to the side, allowing everyone entry.

I waited for everyone to go ahead of me, then walked behind the last blue wolf, nodding at Olson as I passed him.

For once he extended the common curtesy, nodded, and almost smiled. Almost.

I stepped through the portal and onto soft sand; the transition was uneventful apart from the desert heat as it stole my breath. I ensured the weapons were still in place and shielded my eyes from the burning sun with my arm.

Olson came in behind me, closing the portal. He, too, squinted at the brightness.

The sun pelted down on us as we traversed on hot sand toward a lonely pyramid. I was expecting the pyramid to be one of the more well-known structures, instead it stood like a lonely island in a sandstorm.

Glancing at our surroundings, I saw no other buildings or people. I wouldn't be able to confirm whether we were near Egypt. For all I knew, we could've been in Dubai or some other desert.

"Where are we?" I asked Olson as he joined me at the back.

"We're a few miles south of Cairo," he said, not offering any other information.

"Do you know how long we have to retrieve the amulet?"

"Time moves slowly in the Empress's world. What feels like an hour here is only a minute there. So, we have time. But no later than nightfall," he said gravely.

He looked me in the eye and for a moment, time stood still. We shared an understanding that if we failed, the Empress would die, and her world would collapse. That their world would collapse.

"Understood," I finally said when he glanced away and walked ahead of me.

The blue wolves stopped outside the main first entrance

of the pyramid. The doorjamb was large enough for that one-eyed giant to crawl through.

I veered to the side and glimpsed a second entrance small enough for a little person to walk through. Glancing up, I noted a ledge right at the top with a small window.

"Is this Firoze's pyramid?" I whispered.

"This is his home," Olson said, crouching.

When the other wolves crouched low, I did the same.

Olson's ears twitched as if hearing something. Considering I was the only one still in my human form, I wondered whether I should turn into my tiger. My hearing was better if I was in my tiger form; right now I heard nothing.

"Get lower," Olson whispered and pulled on my shirt.

I fell to my stomach, correcting the sword at my side, ensuring it didn't hurt me.

"Shouldn't I shift?"

"Not yet. We want the element of surprise on our side," Olson said, surveying the area like a trained soldier.

I'd been on enough missions to know when danger was near, and this place was as quiet as a cemetery. There was nothing untoward unless I was missing something important.

I stood up from my lying position and walked to the other side of the pyramid. Olson tried to get my attention, but I waved him away.

I peered around the sharp, stone corner of the pyramid and there was nothing but sand and heat.

Sweat peppered my forehead and dripped down my back. My clothing started sticking to my body, and I wished for an oasis with palm trees, a waterfall, and whiskey.

"There's nobody here," I said nonchalantly as I walked back to the crouching wolves, hidden daggers. "I don't know what your wolfie senses are telling you, but I sense nothing."

Olson harrumphed and stood straight, lifting his blue, furry chin. "Four of you go inside and check. The rest wait out here," he said.

Four male blue wolves entered the pyramid as silently as possible. I heard faint calls as they secured each floor and corner. After about thirty minutes, I noted one blue arm waving at us from the top window.

"This place is a decoy, Olson. Isn't there another place he'd hide?" I asked, glancing in the direction we had originally come from. I noted the wind had already blown away our footprints and changed the landscape.

When Olson didn't answer my question, I turned to look at him. Olson and the others stared with glazed over expressions. But the blue arm continued waving from the window.

The hairs on the back of my neck stood on end.

The other presence left me unaffected.

The blue wolves dropped their weapons, collapsed to the ground, and fell asleep. They huddled beside each other like a puppy pile of blue wolfies. It would've been adorable if it wasn't the sinister force rendering them useless so easily.

Olson's expression twisted as he tried to fight the dark hold on him, but he was losing. The darkness forced Olson onto his knees, his eyes clouded over from lavender to black, then white.

Olson's face turned in my direction, but I could tell it wasn't Olson doing it. That whoever had its claws on Olson was inside of him.

"You must be the tiger she sent," said a deep baritone, using Olson's mouth. "It would be easier for me to kill you where you stand, but that wouldn't be fair. I doubt the witch has told you the true story."

When I frowned, the person using Olson as a conduit frowned with me. When Olson glowed, I stepped farther away from him and the blue wolves. I wasn't sure what was happening and didn't want to be in the vicinity when it happened.

"Did she tell you I was afraid of tigers?" said the demon with Olson's mouth.

"She did." I stepped farther away.

Olson glowed brighter, blurring around the edges, and when he became two people, I took another step farther back.

The second person emerged out of Olson's body, that then crumpled to the ground like a rag doll.

The demon morphed into a man with black hair and eyes, and dark brown skin. Power pulsed off his body, and I wished I was a wizard so I could protect myself from this scary Egyptian.

Chapter Seven

I blinked, and my world darkened. I held out my arms to steady myself, and the world changed around me.

My tiger didn't appreciate the sudden movement and pushed his way to the front. We shifted quickly and elegantly, landing on four legs. My ripped clothing fell to the floor like confetti. And my tiger stretched our lithe body and yawned as if he'd been asleep for years.

"Easy kitty," the Egyptian said with panic in his tone. "I didn't bring you here to hurt you." He sneezed and stepped farther back.

I turned my attention on my prey and stalked him. My stomach made unearthly sounds; we were starving.

When Firoze backed himself into a corner, I growled and closed the distance, making rasping sounds.

This man was a little skinny, but a light snack before I found something with more meat on its bones would do just fine.

"That's enough," he said and sneezed again. One side of his face started swelling. "Please, can we talk for a moment?" He said before his lips swelled. "Peese," he mumbled.

I growled and stopped.

On the swollen side of Firoze's face, blisters formed and popped. As each open wound bled, he cried out while searching for something on his body.

I couldn't attack an unarmed man no matter how much fun it would be. He was clearly in a lot of pain. His face was swelling, and the sores were already starting to pus.

What the Empress had said was true; he was highly allergic to me. I didn't have to do much to affect him, either. By standing in front of him as my tiger would do the trick.

Though I was curious as to the reason he hadn't attacked or killed me first. He disarmed Olson and the wolves within seconds, yet he knew I was a tiger and could kill him but did nothing about it.

So far, he had done nothing but bring me here. He didn't seem violent, but then again, one couldn't be too careful.

Firoze found what he was searching for, an injection from his pocket, and stabbed himself in the ass.

Seconds ticked by and his swollen body slowly started normalizing, but he remained in the corner, catching his breath.

When minutes passed and his shaking subsided, he glanced up at me with a pained expression. He swallowed hard and nodded, as if agreeing on his next move.

"Please," — he licked dry lips, — "can we first talk before you shake your body hair all over me and kill me once and for all."

I laughed, but it came out of my toothy jaw like I was choking on hair.

Not wanting to kill him yet, I agreed and shifted back

into my human form. I was comfortable walking around naked but didn't think my host would appreciate discussing important matters with my cock sticking out. Although the distraction could assist me when the time came and I needed to shift again. I could bite his tender neck without much effort.

Unfortunately, my clothing had shredded when I shifted and couldn't wear any of it.

Firoze moved carefully around me and opened a closet. "As much as I welcome nudity, I don't think you want to remain like that while we have our chat," he said with a smirk and handed me a sandy-colored ankle-length gown.

Considering Firoze was alone in his pyramid, he was respectful and not once looked at my crotch area.

"There, that's better," Firoze continued. He sucked in deep breaths of air and approached a chair near a desk and sat behind it. "Please, sit." He pointed at another chair across from him.

He wiped sweat off his brow and drank water from a glass. He filled his glass with more water and offered me something to drink.

I declined his offer, although I was parched. I dressed in the Galabiya he had offered and surveyed my surroundings for danger, but there was nobody else in the dank room but us.

Firoze poured me a glass of water anyway and emptied his glass a second time. He opened a drawer on his right-hand side, pulled out another injection, and placed it on a box in front of him.

I sat down and crossed my right leg over my left, my right knee touching the antique wooden desk. I neatened the dress over my knee. This was my first time wearing a "dress" for men and it was surprisingly comfortable. I wouldn't go out of my way and buy one, though.

With the excitement over, I took the time to admire the surroundings. Adorned on the walls hung beautifully engraved torches, bathing the room in a soft light for a romantic evening. But this encounter was anything but romantic.

To my far left was a closed wooden door with engraved steel reinforcement. It reminded me of hand carved doors fit for a castle.

"Where are we?" I asked.

"A safe place away from the witch. Does she still call herself Empress?" He asked, his tone sarcastic.

"Yep, are you the evil lover who stole her amulet after he murdered her?" I continued surveying the room for danger, but there was nothing. That didn't mean I would let my guard down.

Firoze leaned back in his chair and exhaled loudly. He rubbed the bridge of his nose and closed his eyes, exhaling loudly once more and steepled his fingers. He opened his eyes and stared at me with a pained expression.

"There is so much I could tell you about our dear Empress," he said sarcastically again. "But some of the stories are not mine to tell. I will, however, hand back the amulet I stole." He glanced at the box on his table. "I only took it to save my life."

"You were expecting me… us?"

"How could I not? She's been threatening to harm me for years and vowed to curse me tonight," — he waved his hands in the air, — "with that stupid eclipse."

"She says it's you who cursed her, and she needs the amulet back tonight in order to break the curse."

Firoze burst out laughing, dusting imaginary tears from

his eyes. "She is imaginative. I'll give her that. What's your name?"

"Jude."

"Right, how ironic. Much like Judas Iscariot; the one who betrayed Jesus. Like I was the one who betrayed her. It's more like she is the one…" He shook his head. "Never mind, what's done is done. If all you want is the amulet, here," — he handed me the box, — "take it and tell her to leave me alone. I'm done with her childish games."

Firoze sounded agitated and tired, and for some strange reason I believed him. I felt no sinister power pulsing off of him, and I was sure he could've killed me when he had the chance, but he didn't.

He wanted me to hear his side; a story that sounded like a lover's quarrel. I didn't like it one bit. There were better ways they could've handled this.

"What really happened between you two?" I asked, opening the box and glimpsing at the stunning Heart Scarab amulet. It was perfect; not a scratch on it.

"Never touch it," he said. "It's filled with her evil." He jerked his chin in the box's direction. "She wore it when she tried to kill me. I couldn't allow her to use it, so I took it and hid, but she found me and trapped me here."

Firoze abruptly stood up and paced. "Then, when I heard rumors of what I allegedly did; I knew I had no chance against her. She's powerful, much more powerful than she lets on, so if I were you, I'd be careful. Watch your back." He warned. "And don't trust anyone."

He pointed a long bony finger at me, and I could've sworn I saw blue sparks at the tip of his nail.

"And if she wanted this so badly, she could've taken it from me ten years ago. Maybe now I'll be able to live freely and finally be done with her."

Firoze opened his mouth to say something when the wooden door opened and slammed against the wall. Olson stormed into the room first with three blue wolves behind him.

I stood to stop them from attacking, but it was too late. The blue wolves blasted their fae power directly at Firoze, hitting his chest. He flew into the wall behind him and crumpled to the floor like a rag doll, unmoving.

"What do you think you're doing?" Olson barked and stalked Firoze. "You're fraternizing with the enemy instead of destroying him like she tasked you."

"Now hold on a minute, Olson," I said, raising my hands.

One female stood beside me, half shielding me with her body.

"I almost killed him when I shifted into my tiger, and he already gave me the amulet. You didn't have to kill him. You could've simply used your words instead of flexing your blue hairy muscles."

If Olson wasn't so blue, I was sure he was turning red with anger.

The female moved completely in front of me, blocking Olson's view of my chest.

Olson jerked his chin at her, but she shook her head.

"Is the man dead?" I asked, changing the subject. It was obvious he was dead; blood pooled beneath him, and his head fell to one side. But I wanted Olson to focus on something else instead of me, and to calm down.

"Of course, he is. I did your job for you."

"Listen, I'm not here to fight with you. All I'm saying is he had already given me the amulet. We won. And we were just talking—"

"What did he tell you?"

"He didn't have a chance because you blew in here like the Wicked Witch of the West." I peered around the female's body and pointed at his hands. "With blue electricity coming out of your hands, killing him before he could say anything."

The female wolf stepped closer to me and touched my legs through the dress and held my thighs. I wondered if she was going to push me out of the way or frisk me.

I grabbed her arms and pulled her closer, leaning my elbows on her shoulders and rested my chin on her head. My little bodyguard was short and if Olson tried to kill me, his blue electricity could still strike my shoulder and near my heart, missing her pretty head. But I appreciated her protection, anyway.

Olson exhaled and seemed to visibly calm down. "We must head back," he said. "The eclipse is starting, and she needs us. Hand me the box." Olson held out his furry paw, and I slapped the box into his hand with enough force I was sure it hurt his palm. He didn't flinch.

"I'm not done with you yet," Olson promised and stormed out of the room.

I stared dumbstruck at his back at what had just happened.

"Grumpy, isn't he?" I said to my tiny blue wolf shield. "And who are you?"

"Carrie."

Chapter Eight

"Why did you protect me?" I asked, following my tiny bodyguard through the maze of the pyramid.

"None of this is your fight, and I couldn't allow an innocent to get hurt," Carrie said. "I wasn't sure if Olson would hurt you, but I had to be sure. The Empress said something to him in private—"

"Probably to kill Firoze if I failed."

"Probably."

"Thanks for saving me," I said, squeezing her shoulder.

"Any time," she said, smiling.

We exited out of the ground a few meters away from the pyramid; our sneaky host didn't trust anyone and created his rooms within secret compartments within the pyramid. No wonder the blue wolves couldn't locate him when they first searched the pyramid.

But then again, by Olson's behavior and the quick way he ended Firoze, I couldn't blame him for being paranoid. I was becoming paranoid, and something told me not to trust Olson either.

The only person I could trust was this tiny blue wolf leading me out of the slaughterhouse. Carrie was the only blue wolf with light brown hair and blue streaks. The other wolves all had dark brown or black hair. I wondered if there was anything else different about her; perhaps a third breast or a split tongue.

A grin split my face in two thinking naughty thoughts and relieved nobody saw me.

As if hearing my thoughts, Carrie glanced over her shoulder and winked at me.

Yep, she read something all right.

Carrie stopped, and I almost walked into her. Up ahead stood Olson near the open portal like a madman, ushering the blue wolves through with violence.

"What's his problem?" I mumbled softly.

"He just wants to get home," Carrie answered.

"Is he always like this?"

"No," she said, shaking her head. "But ever since the Empress…"

I had to know more when Carrie left her sentence hanging. I thought if she didn't see Olson and forced her to look at me, then perhaps she'd open up to me about what was going on.

"What, Carrie? What don't you want to say?" I asked, my eyes flitting to Olson; he continued yanking the blue wolves one at a time through the portal. From what I could tell, nobody wanted him touching them.

"Quick, we have little time."

"I'd suggest you two love birds hurry if you want to get home. It's a long flight back to Sterling Meadow." Olson said in a sinister tone.

"It's nothing," Carrie said, looking nervously over her

shoulder. "Let's go before he closes the portal. I'll tell you later in private."

I nodded, and we approached the portal in silence.

Olson stood guard, wearing a hostile expression that left me nervous.

Just as we reached him, he darted inside, and the portal closed.

"What the hell?" I yelled, pushing Carrie to the side as I reached for the closing doorway. It closed, Olson grinned, and it popped in my face like a balloon. "I can't believe he just did that. What an asshole!"

"Shit," Carrie mumbled, surveying the area. "We're far away from Cairo and if I remember correctly, there's nothing out here. He has just doomed us to die out here."

"You're part fae, aren't you? Don't you have the same magic?"

"No," she said as she continued glancing around for something. There was nothing else here except for the pyramid. "We all have something different," she said, looking at me. "And as you guessed correctly, I read minds, but Olson is the most powerful and the only one who creates portals."

"And you couldn't read his mind before he closed the portal?"

"The blue wolves can block each other from our various gifts," she said, annoyingly. "When I see him again, I will give him a piece of my mind." She slammed her fist into her palm and winced.

Without saying a word, she headed back toward the secret tunnel to Firoze's rooms. Not wanting to wait out here alone, I followed her; somebody had to protect her from herself. She seemed determined to do something, and I wanted to be there in case she made a mistake.

Once we were back in Firoze's chamber, we searched his

desk for something; anything. There was a handful of ticket stubs and a diary. I picked up the satchel from the floor and slipped the diary inside.

The sword and dagger they gave me weighed me down and I wanted to leave it here. Something told me to hold on to it, though. If we were to walk in the desert, there could be demons, and I had to keep us safe. Carrie didn't have many powers, while I only had my beast I could change into.

I searched the closet while Carrie went through the cabinet.

"Find anything?" I asked, finding nothing but clothing.

"I'd like to read that diary you carefully slipped inside the satchel. Otherwise, no, there's nothing. Now where do you think he slept? There were no other rooms, and I don't see a bed anywhere."

"Let's explore the rest of his secret hallway. Maybe we'll find something."

I took the lead, and we traversed the narrow hallway we hadn't seen before. The tight stone corridor veered left and right, up and down, and seemed to spiral upward. There were no other rooms and as we searched, we placed our hands on the walls for a secret door. There was nothing.

When the pathway made a sharp U-turn and continued downward, a knot formed in the pit of my stomach.

"I don't like this," Carrie whispered behind me, and reached for my linen dress.

I grabbed her hand for her comfort, and she huddled closer against me.

The torch in my hand revealed a dark passage with water dripping from the ceiling. I surmised we were underground, with water above us. Which made little sense since we were in a desert, and I'd seen no water within miles of the pyramid.

"I agree," Carrie said, reading my mind. "Nothing makes sense. Look!" She pointed at a light up ahead and we approached with caution.

Once we reached the light, I shielded my eyes from the brightness. The torch in my hand extinguished itself when a blast of cold air struck us, stealing my breath.

Snowflakes fell on my face as we exited the tunnel, and I shivered.

"What in the hell...?" I gawked at the mounds of snow before us. "I don't understand."

"It appears he was the cursed one and not the Empress." Carrie shivered behind me and huddled closer.

Carrie said what I thought. This was what Firoze had meant when he said he wanted to be done with her childish games. She had placed him in some sort of maze.

As if answering my question, the snow disappeared, and was replaced with a large room adorned with gold furnishings. The gold was so bright it hurt my eyes.

There was a large bath in the center of the room, filled with white liquid.

Carrie stood beside me and gasped.

The pool rippled.

A strange smell assaulted my nose, but I couldn't place it.

I stepped backward but collided with the wall; our doorway was now closed.

Carrie stood behind me. Her fearless streak seemed to have melted with the snow.

We watched as the water rippled with an object just beneath the surface.

Then the object broke through the surface, rising like dark nightmare.

Chapter Nine

I watched in horror as the object in the white liquid morphed into the Empress like a night terror. The thick milky liquid dripped teasingly down her naked body; I couldn't tear my eyes away.

"Empress?" Carrie whispered. She glanced at me, shaking her head as if this was the first time she'd seen the Empress this way.

The Empress slowly climbed up the two steps out of the milky liquid and headed toward us, but when she saw Carrie, something flashed in her features I couldn't decipher.

I didn't want to admit it, but the Empress was stunning. Her pert nipples were ready for sucking and biting; her breasts were round and firm, while her slender waist and hips were every man's wet dream; I'd love nothing more than to lick whatever slick slit was between her legs and then cum all over her toned stomach.

I imagined she tasted like sweet nectar which dripped down the inside of her muscular thighs. And in that moment, I wanted to thrust my hard cock deep inside of her and make her scream my name.

I blinked when air popped in my face and the sensual thoughts washed over me like a cold shower.

The Empress grinned naughtily and continued staring at me as if removing my clothing with her dark gaze.

Carrie shifted uncomfortably beside me, breaking the Empress' concentration, and she scowled at Carrie.

Carrie averted her eyes and pushed me in front of her.

"What's going on?" I asked, even though I knew what was going on. I still wanted the Empress to explain.

She cackled like a witch, making me flinch. "You aren't the brightest, are you, little Jude? My striped kitty-cat. Purr for me?" The Empress said with a condescending smile.

I swallowed hard but held my ground. I didn't know the extent of her powers or what her intensions were. Either way, she was dangerous and I should not give in to her.

The Empress stared hungrily at me, but I dared not look away. I suspected she hoped her naked body and the salacious thoughts she gave me would entice me, but it didn't; there was something off-putting about her. Although I had dirty thoughts about her, I never wanted to do any of them with her.

A shadow moved across the room. My eyes flitted in the direction it had come from. But it was the blood moon moving in front of the sun, almost eclipsing it, that held my attention.

I shouldn't have looked away from the Empress. In one breath, she was in front of me, with one hand holding my chin, the other grabbing my flaccid cock. She sniffed near my chin, and when her eyes found Carrie, she hissed.

"Go before I eat your heart directly out of your chest," the Empress said.

Carrie darted for the door on the other side of the room, and exited without looking back at me.

Chicken. I thought, but silently hoping she was getting help.

"Now I have you all to myself," the Empress breathed near my ear, causing all the hairs on my neck and arms to stand at attention; and not pleasantly. It was a pity my cock wasn't responding to her; she seemed the type to take offense.

"Why don't you like me, Jude?" she asked, almost sounding normal. *Almost.*

"Well, for one, you're grabbing my balls like you own them. I distinctly remember not leaving them here for you to lock away. So, if you don't mind giving them back." I grabbed the hand holding my cock and carefully pried her fingers off me and stepped out of her grasp. I sucked in a fresh breath and moved farther away from her.

"Nice place," I said. I tried not to turn my back on her as I moved around the room, and away from her. "But all this gold is blinding. I'm amazed you can still see."

"Yes, well, someone like me needs pretty things," she purred. "And you, Jude, are pretty. Would you like to sit on my wall?" She asked teasingly.

I hoped she was teasing.

The Empress moved seductively, swaying her naked hips as she followed me. Her neatly waxed mound was tempting, but my cock was uninterested in a female who wanted to eat us.

My beast didn't want her either and growled inside my head. He wanted to be set free so he could eat her first. I had to focus on other things; things not involving sex or her.

"Why have him killed?" I asked when I saw a painting of the Empress and Firoze.

The Empress stopped beside me, slipping her smaller hand in mine; her nails scratched down the inside of my arm before she gripped my hand. A warm liquid dripped down my arm and splashed onto the floor. As much as my arm stung, I didn't want to break eye contact. The Empress was like a snake, ready to strike, if left unattended.

"I no longer needed him," she said curtly, as if she had just cleaned her feet on the carpet.

"Yeah, well, when anyone is done with an ex, we usually just leave them and move on with our lives. We don't bloody them like a pincushion."

The Empress burst out laughing. "You are funny," she added, and leaned her head on my shoulder. "Won't you stay?"

"I'd love to," I said loudly. "But I have a job and friends who are probably looking for me. You know, I'm such a nice guy that I'm actually missed." I wanted to ask if anyone missed her, but I didn't feel like having my eyes gouged out.

"Nobody is looking for you, Jude. I made sure of it."

I frowned.

"Nothing bad, I promise. Just that you left a note saying you're on holiday."

I hoped Flynn realized it was a lie; I needed them to find me. I regretted going into the forest in search of evidence that explained Flynn and Penn's disappearance. I was looking for an alternative scenario to the one that actually happened. Flynn's troubles started when the old shaman needed his beast; their history went back to when Flynn was a boy.

This... the Empress and her world was something different. If only I didn't feel the power in the forest. I should've listened to Flynn and forget about it, but something drew me to the forest, to the portal. I now understand it was the

Empress who had called me there with Olson's help; his portal opening for me at the right time.

I needed to destroy the Empress's world.

"Jude?" The Empress said sternly, bringing me out of my thoughts. "Where did you go?" She asked tenderly. Her fingertips caressing my left cheek; when I focused on her, she smiled. "There you are. Now, where were we…" she stopped her gentle touch and approached a mirror framed with gold.

The Empress combed her fingers through her hair as she stared at herself. The mirror rippled as if her presence alone brought it to life.

"Mirror, mirror," she sang.

Oh boy, I'd seen this movie, and didn't like where it was going.

"Just kidding," she said, looking at me in the mirror. Then she focused on herself again, admiring her beauty.

The one thing I couldn't stand was a vain woman; and certainly not to this extent.

She murmured something only she could hear, and a robe appeared, covering her body. She tied the robe tightly, only revealing her cleavage.

Unfortunately, I'd had the misfortune of seeing everything she had already, and I didn't want any of it.

"Right, now where were we?" she asked, still admiring her beauty in the mirror. "Oh yes," — she snapped her fingers, — "my Heart Scarab amulet." And the item appeared around her neck.

When the Empress turned to look at me. The blood moon eclipsed the sun, and her eyes were as black as night.

Chapter Ten

I didn't know what to expect from the Empress, but I stood my ground, getting ready to shift into my tiger. I would fight her with everything I had. I refused to become a statistic.

The moon bathed the lavish room with its maroon inky-darkness, and humming pierced my eardrum.

The Empress's eyes darkened, her feet shifted into strong claws like a falcon, and another set of arms appeared beneath her other two.

When the humming turned into hissing, the Empress's dark hair twirled into thick strands and moved. The tiny heads of the poisonous snakes pointed their tasting tongues in my direction, and my tiger roared in my head.

I shifted into my tiger when the Empress reached for me, her mouth opening wide with two rows of sharp teeth.

"Come here, tiger," she hissed menacingly. "I hate working for what I want." She stalked me like the predator she was, and I didn't want to become her fodder.

"I'm not that easy, Empress," I said through my large,

toothy jaw and backed up, searching for a way out of her nightmare room.

"I want to add you to my collection," she said, raising her four arms and posed as if presenting herself as a gift.

I cocked my head to the side, not understanding her reference.

"When I consume a special type of supernatural, I absorb a part of them and it reflects on my body." The snakes hissed, her sharp claws extended and tapped on the floor, and one set of hands rested on her hips.

"You kill shifters, and they became a part of you."

She nodded. Her snakes hissed and moved like thick dreadlocks on her head.

"I'm cursed but this happened many years ago," she said. Then like the time in the tavern, visions of her memory floated near her like a movie as she spoke.

"I was a young Queen in Ancient Egypt, and he was a powerful priest-physician. He wanted more while I grew bored. And as I curled my fingers around his neck," — one set of hands throttled thin air in front of her, — "he invoked Heka. He spoke words I had never heard before and left me ill prepared. And when he died in my arms," — she pointed at her clawed feet, — "this is what I got in return. And with each lover I smothered, I absorbed a part of him."

The Empress neared and her childlike features returned, along with her thick dark hair. She seemed so innocent and pure. My dominant side pushed to the surface, and I wanted to protect her; to keep her safe. But this was a facade. She killed easily.

"Not only did I get a piece of them," she continued nonchalantly, and her snakes returned. "But a piece of their soul and their power, too." Her eyes brightened like powerful stars at midnight, but her sinister smile revealed sharp teeth. Her sudden change in demeanor was unsettling.

Something to my right blurred past me.

I snarled at the object and the Empress. I didn't want to become dinner and couldn't trust whoever had joined us.

The object stopped in the dark corner.

The Empress turned so she could see me and the newcomer.

The object moved out of the shadows, its yellow eyes glowed brightly, then its blue fur emerged.

"Olson, how kind of you to join us," the Empress purred. Her words were smooth like silk and dangerously seductive.

Olson, in his giant blue wolf, snarled at the Empress.

Another blue blur dashed inside the room to stand beside Olson.

"Olson?" The Empress asked with concern in her tone. "What's the meaning of this?"

"You misled us, Empress," Olson said, but his furry jaw barely moved. "You tricked us." His accusatory yellow eyes flitted to her four arms and strange claw-like-feet. "You are an abomination and collector of shifter souls."

"There's so much you don't understand," the Empress said sadly.

Again, memory-visions floated beside the Empress as she revealed that if she killed a lover at the blood-moon eclipse every ten years, her powers doubled.

When her eyes flitted in my direction I glanced away. I didn't want her to think there was any chance with me. I would fight her every step of the way.

Then her memory-visions showed how she chose her lovers carefully based on their strength. And when she returned to the world she'd created for herself, she took time to heal after each murder, and to get used to the new appendage. She would practice how to use the newly given power and as time went on more lonely creatures joined her.

There were creatures living in her world I hadn't seen when I had first arrived because that's how they preferred it; apart from the tiny faeries and the one eyed giant, there were forest creatures, leprechauns, and goblins to name a few.

The memory-visions continued showing the arrival of Olson and his blue wolves. How they stumbled upon her portal, and they too found solace with the Empress.

But she lied about why she had created her world and why she needed the amulet; which brought no power to her. It was a gimmick for the blue wolves to retrieve and for Olson to kill Firoze.

"Firoze was my true love," she said sadly. "I couldn't kill him myself because he had nothing to offer. His power was weak, and it would lessen my powers. Olson had to do it for me." She glanced at Olson with her childlike expression, and I hoped Olson saw through her illusion.

"And I needed you," — the Empress turned her attention on me, — "to feel like the hero that you are. I needed you to help them."

"To help the allusion of it all," I said unhappily.

Because the Empress instructed Olson to leave me at the pyramid and to find my way to her room where she awaited. But she wasn't counting on Carrie being with me.

The Empress's memory-vision popped as her story ended where we all stood, waiting for someone to do something first.

Not wanting to wait any longer, I lunged into the air and

went straight for the amulet. The Empress may have shown us what she wanted us to see but I didn't trust her. The amulet may still provide the Empress with Firoze's power, and I wanted to try and neutralize her.

"No!" The Empress shrieked and tried to throw me off her. Four powerful hands gripped my body, but I was quicker. I yanked the amulet from her neck and held onto it with my firm jaw. The nervous look in her eyes told me that there was power in the amulet that she fed off of.

Something stung my side, and I lost my footing, crashing to the floor limply instead of on my feet. My side continued to sting, but at least I had the amulet.

The Empress' shriek echoed inside the room.

I cringed, it felt as though my ears would bleed.

The white liquid in her bath sloshed and messed on the floor. Her golden framed mirror swung on the wall, fell, and crashed onto the floor, breaking into a million tiny pieces.

Olson and the blue wolf lunged for the Empress at the same time; Olson grabbed her neck; the other wolf went for her clawed legs.

The trio fought but the Empress couldn't shake the two blue wolves off of her. Olson bit down harder, and the other wolf tore at the Empress' legs while biting her clawed feet.

The Empress' shrieks ended when Olson crushed her windpipe. Her wild snaky hair bit into Olson one head at a time, but he seemed to feel nothing. He continued biting her neck until her arms dropped to her sides and her snakes fell limply around her head.

Blood blossomed beneath her body, leaking into the bath until the white liquid turned pink.

My side continued to throb, and I spat out the amulet to lick my wounds.

The blue wolf who attacked the Empress' leg came to

me and helped clean the snake bite. Whatever was in the blue wolf's saliva helped and the poison seeped out of the wound and onto the floor.

I gagged when I saw the green/brown poison near my paws, but was relieved it was out of my system. "Thank you," I said as I shifted back into my human form.

The blue wolf smiled as they, too, shifted back. Carrie sat naked beside me and my tiger howled; which forced me to howl at her.

Carrie laughed and hugged me. "Someone is feeling better," she said with a giggle.

My cock chose that moment to stand at attention. It was the worst time to have an erection but I couldn't help it, Carrie had that effect on me.

"Oh my," Carrie said, staring at my hard member. "Is that all for me?" She asked teasingly.

"Well, it's yours if you want," I said with a grin. I wanted to lie back and allow her access to every part of my body but not now, not here, not like this.

"I accept the invitation but not here," she said what I was thinking, and side-eyeing Olson.

Olson cleared his throat.

Carrie stopped making love to my cock with her eyes and stood at attention for her leader.

I climbed to my feet, coughed into my hand, and thought of boring things and not Carrie naked. "Thank you for saving me," I said, realizing the full extent of Olson's power. He was truly a potent wolf when he tore into her flesh, killing her. "Or your Empress would've had my striped tail by now, and then next week she would most likely be covered in blue fur."

"I suspect the amulet was the source of her true power," Olson said gravely. "Thank you for risking your life and taking it out of her hands, making her easy to destroy. She never behaved like she did today, and she was good to us in the beginning," he said sadly. "I'm disappointed, but I now see how she used us to do everything for her. And she used me the most, because without me, my wolves wouldn't have done what she asked."

I understood how Olson felt, being used and toyed with cut deeply. And I suspected it was worse for Olson because he loved her.

"Don't blame yourself," Carrie said, squeezing his shoulder. "We all felt safe with her, and we wanted to help her. But she had ulterior motives and would use anyone to get what she wanted. So, don't beat yourself up. We survived."

Olson smiled but it didn't reach his eyes. "Let's get you home," he said to me. He nodded curtly, turned on his heel and left the room. But before he exited, he pulled the Empress' body into the pink liquid, lit a match, and threw it inside. The liquid caught flames and burned.

Carrie and I ran after Olson. Once we exited her palace, we stood far away to watch it burn to the ground.

"How did you know it was flammable?" I asked Olson when we walked back to the town where the rest of the wolves waited.

"Couldn't you smell it?"

"Smell what?" I asked, shaking my head. When I thought about it, I added, "I smelled something when we first entered."

"I smelled nothing," Carrie added.

"When I entered all I smelled was fuel. It's as if she drank the stuff. Anyway, I thought it best to burn her body than to chop her up and dispose of her."

I cringed, relieved it wasn't necessary. The last thing I

wanted to do was chop anyone up and then dispose of the parts. My name was not Dexter, although it was a great show.

"Now what?" Carrie asked, staring at me with a naughty grin.

Chapter Eleven

I sat across from Carrie and watched. Slowly, teasingly, she removed her top, freeing her large supple breasts; they were more than a handful each, and my cock strained against my pants, eager for release.

Carrie's luscious grin and the need in her eyes was the end of me. I stood up from my chair, but she raised her hand, stopping me.

"Sit," she demanded, and I complied reluctantly, shifting my cock to the other side, and pulling up my pants as I sat down again.

My beast stirred awake, smelling the female's scent. He roared frustratingly in my head, and I didn't blame him. I wanted to roar myself.

Carrie caressed her skin as she moved her right hand slowly over her right breast, pinching her nipple. Then her fingers walked down her stomach, toward that naked mound.

"Sweet Jesus," I mumbled to myself when her fingers slipped inside her tight pussy.

I darted to my feet, ripped off my clothing, and stood between Carrie's wide-open legs. She grinned up at me with hooded eyes, and I wanted to fuck her hard and make her moan.

"Lost patience?"

"Fuck patience, I want you now." I leaned forward with my hands on the wall.

Carrie strained to look up at me. Finally, she slipped out from under me and bounced on my bed. Once on her back, she opened her legs wide, inviting me with a crooked finger.

I didn't wait and stalked my prey. My beast anxious to taste our blue wolf beauty. I crawled onto the bed and settled between her legs. I pressed my cock against her wet spot and nudged inside; her heated sheath taking all of me.

I loved that initial moment when I pushed inside of her and her mouth parted, gasping as I filled her. Her eyes rolled into the back of her head when I continued thrusting inside of her, and pleasurable goosebumps covered my skin.

It must've been two minutes later when our orgasms struck us at the same time. Carrie scratched my back, and I came inside of her. She mumbled something unintelligibly and I chalked it up to a great orgasm and she was thanking her gods.

I slipped out of her and fell onto my back, pulling her against my side. Our bodies were covered in a thin layer of sweat, and I enjoyed having her snuggle beside me. I kissed the top of her head, exhaled and closed my eyes; enjoying the moment.

"Did you read Firoze's diary?" Carrie blurted in the silence.

My eyes shot open, not expecting this conversation now and especially not after our lovemaking.

After we destroyed the Empress and her double story

home yesterday, her world started crumbling around us. We escaped the collapsing world with all the creatures in time.

Once we returned to Sterling Meadow's Forest, Olson closed the portal permanently. With nowhere to go, I suggested they remain in the forest while I spoke with Léon, Master Vampire of our town, and my boss.

After I arrived back at the warehouse, it relieved everybody I was alive and well. They knew the note the Empress had left for them was faked, and they had continued their daily search of the forest; but the portal had remained hidden.

When Léon arrived, I explained what had happened, and he agreed to allow the creatures to live in the forest. They were welcome to move to the city if they wished.

The blue wolves were in talks with Shawn, who remembered Olson from the Retreat. There might be space for all the blue wolves within Shawn's were-wolf pack, which included housing and the possibilities of jobs.

Everyone was settling in.

I was having a good time with Carrie, until she mentioned the diary.

"What's wrong?" she asked, letting go of me and leaning on her elbow to look at me. "You're scaring me, Jude."

I patted her bum. "It's okay," — I said, sitting up and scooting off the bed, — "his diary was filled with nonsense, and it's been destroyed."

"What? Why?" She asked, clearly unhappy about the decision I'd made without her.

I stared down at her, my nostrils flaring, and pursed my lips.

She submitted and averted her eyes.

"It was the best thing to do under the circumstances.

Apart from the nonsense he wrote, he left incantations that if it landed in the wrong hands, could spell disaster for supernaturals." What I omitted; it was particularly disastrous for the blue wolves.

As I read Firoze's diary last night, my gut told me to destroy it. The incantations detailed how to destroy various supernaturals at their DNA level, turning them into a human.

I didn't know much about biology, but my gut instinct warned me that Firoze's magical words rang true. So, I burned the journal.

Carrie sat up and scooted off the bed to join me. I exhaled a shaky breath and pulled her closer.

"It's going to be all right," I said and kissed her forehead. "Everybody is safe. Let's enjoy our time together and see where it takes us?"

Carrie nodded in my embrace and held on to me like her life depended on it.

"What should we do today?" I asked, slowly letting go. "I have some time before my shift starts."

Carrie grinned and headed for the bathroom. She disappeared and the shower turned on.

"Join me?" She said with a seductive tone.

I didn't need a second invitation and joined her.

Chapter Twelve

LÉON'S MISSING ARTIFACT

I paced up and down, holding my hands behind my back with my head up high, and schooling my features. What I wanted to do was bite into each of the shifters' necks who worked in my warehouse, but they were lucky that I enjoyed their company enough not to hurt a hair on their body. Unfortunately, if I did bite any of them, I would have all sorts of hell on my doorstep from the various shifter clans.

"We're sorry, Léon," Kai said nervously. He glanced over his shoulder at his mate, Naomi, who averted her eyes.

"With all the security features we have and not one, but four powerful shifters guarding my artifacts, how can someone break in and steal from me?" I asked as anger coursed through my hard, black veins.

I stopped beside the destroyed wooden crate that held an artifact that nobody should ever have known about. Nobody knew, not even my brother, Sebastian. Yet it was now in someone else's hands. I tapped my long fingernails against the broken pieces of the crate, the sound echoing in the large warehouse.

Lee, Flynn, and Jude looked just as guilty as Kai.

"Why was the back door unlocked?" I asked, staring at Jude.

Jude slowly glanced up at me, as if sensing my dark gaze. "I was cleaning the kitchen, again, and I must've forgotten—"

"Forgotten!" I yelled. "None of you understand the gravity of the situation we find ourselves in." I sucked in a breath even though I'd never needed to. "And why are these females living here? I never said they could." I pointed at the three ladies who recently moved in; Penn, Natalie, and Carrie.

Lee stood up and raised his hand respectfully. "If I may, Léon, I apologize on behalf of my shifter-brothers for not seeking your approval. We didn't think it was necessary, but I understand your concern."

"Thank you, Lee. I accept your apology. Well, since the females are here, they might as well work. I'm sure you can dust and clean?" I said, waiting for one of them to complain, but they didn't.

Carrie raised her head as if wanting to comment, but Jude shook his head. I knew Carrie was a blue wolf and could fight her own battles. The other two females were Komodo dragon shifters. They could come in handy, too. Unfortunately, Naomi was too human, even though Kai had changed her into a were-leopard. She could do the cooking and cleaning.

I stopped pacing and stood before my shifter-minions, my anger slowly receding. "I'm sure you're wondering what they stole," I said, then continued without waiting for them to answer. "As you know, I import quite a few items from Egypt, Africa, and even South America. Some artifacts are priceless, others are sentimental, but this item is religious and whoever broke in knew that it was here."

Something squeaked near my feet, and the shifters readied to attack. I pushed the crate with my foot, revealing an opening in the ground. My frown deepened.

"They came through the floor," Flynn said, approaching cautiously.

I kicked the wooden crate away and hissed. The sand moved when something scurried away.

"They came through the sewage tunnel running beneath the warehouse," Jude said, standing beside Flynn. Both men stared at the hole in the floor like it was the first time seeing such a thing.

Kai told the females to stand back while he and Lee closed the gap, but females being females, they didn't listen and approached with their mates. I wanted to roll my eyes but didn't. If they wanted to join their men in searching for whatever that was, I wouldn't stop them.

I slammed my heel into the ground, and the floor cracked open. I continued kicking at the tiles until more chipped away. When the hole was big enough, I crouched down.

"Are you coming with us?" Lee asked nervously.

I peered up at him and without saying a word; they understood the magnitude of the situation and how important this artifact was.

Lee raised his hands in surrender. "What can we do—"

"Shift into your beasts and help me hunt this creature down. And if the females join, they cannot hold me liable for their injuries."

"We'll be fine," Naomi said, then pursed her lips and slunk behind Kai.

Wasting no time, I jumped down into the recently made

hole and landed in thick water. I splashed drain water over my pants, but it was a small price to pay. I could always buy a new pair.

Two leopards, a lion, a tiger, and a blue wolf joined me in the drain. The three females jumped in after them, neither of them complaining about the smell or that the water ruined their clothing.

"They headed this way," I said, pointing into the darkness.

"I hate this," Kai said through his toothy jaw. "Nobody knows what's really down there."

"Well," Penn said, "there could be crocodiles."

"It's a good thing you and Natalie are with us," I said, walking past them. "Maybe you two can frighten them with your Komodo."

Flynn growled, protecting his mate, then quickly closed his enormous jaw after I glared daggers at him.

"I'm teasing, lion. Besides, whatever is down there, I'm sure I can handle myself, but having company will make this easier and a lot more fun."

I headed into the thick darkness. Although I couldn't see detail in the dark, I could find my way around without a torch. We traversed down the drain and into the bowels of the sewage maze, and I was grateful I could block out the stink.

And having the additional were-animals as back up I was confident I would retrieve the artifact soon.

Chapter Thirteen

DOWN THE DRAIN

I traversed down the sewage tunnel with my army of shifters, and their girlfriends, behind me. This was definitely a new experience for me since I usually did business with vampires, or I hired shifters to do the rest. But this artifact was too important to ask someone else to retrieve for me.

We were close to the centre where all the sewage and stormwater drains merged when I stopped dead. The shifters stopped behind me, and we silently neared the end of our tunnel.

There were distant whispers, scuttling across shallow water and ground, and strange footsteps; footsteps that reminded me of sharp nails clicking against metal.

I stepped carefully to the end of the tunnel, and toward the light, and peered over the edge. There in the center of the drain maze stood creatures I'd only heard about and thought extinct; apart from that one time when Blaire, my girlfriend, and Ralph, her partner, encountered one.

The leader stood on a box, and anger filled my veins.

His hard, curvy fingers with its extra thumb and long nails curled around my artifact.

His eyes were useless and his hairless nose was ringed by 22 elegant fleshy tentacles that looked like a worm orgy was taking place on his face. The tiny tentacles sniffing and tasting the air was unnerving. I wanted to punch him in his face, rip out his heart, and take back what belonged to me.

He screeched his complaint in his animal-speak. I didn't understand his language, but I got the gist of it; they were about to use the artifact.

I didn't know what would happen if these creatures used the artifact, or how it would change them. One thing I did know was that I didn't want to wait and find out.

"We need to stop them," I whispered over my shoulder at my shifter-men. "And they may not use the artifact."

Natalie pushed through the crowd and stood beside me, glancing at the creatures below. She shook her head and looked up at me, her eyes wide as saucers. "Moles?" She mouthed.

"Mole-men, my dear," I whispered. "They are mole-men. I thought Blaire and Ralph destroyed the last one years ago, but it seems they've reproduced."

"How should we do this?" Naomi asked nervously. Lee, her leopard mate, scent marked her and nudged her back.

"I suggest those who have never fought remain here while the others do what they can to destroy them, and I'll get the artifact back. I repeat, nobody goes after the artifact."

"Is that the Holy Grail?" Penn asked, staring at the leader holding my artifact.

"Yes," I said nonchalantly.

"I thought it wasn't real," she said, still mesmerized by the shiny object.

I snapped my fingers in front of her eyes. She flinched and stepped backward.

"Like I was saying," I continued. "I'm the only one who can touch it, or you will end up a zombie chasing something you can never have."

Penn swallowed hard and glanced back at her lion mate. Flynn pushed through his friends and licked her hand.

"Natalie and I can help. Our Komodo dragons are powerful and can destroy most of them," Penn said, readying herself to shift.

"That's what I love to hear," I said, smiling. "Now get ready."

Chapter Fourteen

FIGHT OR FLIGHT

I sensed hesitation from the girls and did my best not to listen in on their thoughts, and instead, jumped down in the polluted waters below.

My yelling as I entered caused the leader to almost drop the Holy Grail. The tall, skinny man with fur covering his body had features similar to that of a mole, like a small human mashed together with a star-nosed mole. He gripped the Holy Grail tighter, clutching it to his furry chest.

Once I landed, I stood straight and stared down at the tiny-mole-creatures closest to me. Then I glanced up. "Hand me the item you stole from me," I said, staring hard at the leader, holding out my right hand.

"No," the leader said, backing up. There was a tunnel I didn't want him reaching or he would disappear. "Attack the vampire!" He screamed and ran.

My shifters joined me below and only Naomi stayed in the tunnel, with Kai standing at the back, protecting her.

Natalie and Penn shifted into their potent Komodo dragons, scaring the mole-men. The two mole-men standing nearest to them pooped from shock. I grinned. At least it stopped them from storming us.

It pleased me to have these ladies part of the team. Their bites were poisonous, and their large body and tail were something to be proud of. They were killing machines I'd gladly employ. I made a mental note to ask their mates, Lee and Flynn, whether I could approach them to join my shifter team. But that would have to wait. Right now, I needed to get my cold, dead hands on that mole-man with my Holy Grail.

I pushed two mole-men out of my way and charged the leader, but he was already close to the tunnel. Fighting erupted behind me, followed by screeching. Something wet hit my back, but I ignored it and bolted for the leader.

I just touched his shoulder when he disappeared down a tunnel. Not wanting him to get away, I jumped down into the tunnel after him. I didn't know where this drop would take me and braced for impact.

The tunnel reminded me of a water ride but without the water, and there were hard pieces sticking out where the tunnel connected, tearing my pants and legs. I was grateful I healed fast, but damn, my pants were being shredded.

When the tunnel leveled out, my momentum slowed. The tunnel opened up into a cement-like-cave and before the leader jumped off I dove for him, slamming into his back, and we crashed to the hard floor.

I rolled with the mole-man and relief washed over me when my fingers felt the cool metal of the Holy Grail. "This belongs to me, creature," I said, yanking on the artifact.

"Please, don't take it away. It's the only thing that can turn us back."

I pushed the mole-man away from me and clutched the Holy Grail against my chest. I levitated farther away from him, readying myself to strike again. "You had no right taking what doesn't belong to you. Now tell me, how did you know I have this?"

The mole-man wiped blood off of his top lip and winced when he felt the bloody scrape against the side of his face. "I'll tell you everything you want to know, but first promise to help us."

"I promise nothing. You don't know what this can do to you, and frankly, I don't want to know. This is a dangerous artifact—"

"It will help us."

"Explain."

Chapter Fifteen

A CURE FOR BLINDNESS

Eddie's star-nose twitched every time he rubbed the wound on the side of his head.

"The more you rub it, the worse it will feel. Just leave it alone," I said, tucking the Holy Grail inside my coat.

Eddie sat back against the cement wall, blindly watching me. "I heard one of your vampires talk about all the artifacts stored in your warehouse. You should be careful who you tell your secrets to."

"Who was it?"

"Help me first and then I'll tell you everything."

I sighed wearily. If I did as he asked and allowed him to sip from the Holy Grail, I didn't know what kind of creature he would turn into. It was a risk I didn't want to take.

"Legend has it that if you sip pure water from this, it will cure you of your illnesses and help knock off a few years." I sighed for effect. "I don't know if it will turn you back into a what? What are you if not a star-nosed mole?"

"I'm human. Just a plain old human male who has been

trying to help those like me," he said, pointing in the general direction of where the others were. I doubted any of them were alive if those two Komodo dragons had their way. "We just want to go back to our human lives."

"Where are you from? I never heard of someone turning humans into mole-men in my town." I was furious. If someone was doing this under my watch, I'd turn the town upside down looking for the person responsible.

"We're from Las Vegas," he said sadly. "And we worked at the same casino. When the previous owners sold the casino, the new owner didn't warn us what would happen if we stayed. We arrived for work the next day and told to go into a room where someone waited for us. The next thing there was gas everywhere and chaos broke out. We hurried to get out, but it was too late. They had turned us into these creatures." He raised his arms and his star-nose twitched.

"Did everyone escape?" I asked, vaguely remembering a story a few years ago about a mole outbreak.

"No, they captured some." Eddie visibly relaxed, but his star-nose continued sniffing. I glanced at the worm wiggling away and no doubt Eddie would eat it if it wasn't for me standing in his way.

"Can you remember anything else?"

Eddie fell silent for a moment, and his nose stopped twitching. "It's been so long, but I remember someone saying they wanted to find a cure for blindness."

"Blindness?" I repeated. The lines between my eyes deepened, and I quickly schooled my features. He was a blind mole and couldn't see me, but I couldn't be too careful. The last thing I needed now was for anyone to know I had emotions.

"Yeah, a witch turned us into star-nosed moles, who

have terrible eyesight, only for them to test on us and see if they could reverse blindness—"

"That's absurd," I said, interrupting him. "I don't understand labs sometimes." I rarely felt annoyed, but this was beyond ridiculous. But then again, idiots with money and egos were everywhere and did stupid things.

"I overheard others saying they were already testing on naked mole-rats and golden moles. Then, once they had the right results, they would destroy us. After we escaped, I heard that lab was destroyed, those responsible were arrested, and the survivors were released into the care of a sanctuary, while we came here in search of a cure."

"And the witch who cursed you couldn't reverse the spell?"

"No, she tried and failed," Eddie said, his nose twitching in my direction. "And then she disappeared." He sat down with a weary sigh and rubbed his sightless eyes.

"How did you hear about my artifact?" I needed to know who had betrayed my trust by searching through my imported records. Nobody knew I had this item since I alone had it shipped to me using my import company, and the person I had dealt with would say nothing.

Eddie fidgeted with the fur on his body and glanced blindly up at me. His star-nose moving around on his face was unnerving.

"I didn't know for sure what it was," he said, sounding guilty. "We listen to everyone in town using these tunnels. It was by chance I overheard your shifters talking about an artifact they had no information on. And after I broke in and felt the power of the Holy Grail in my hands, I knew I had to take it and use it. I don't know if it will work, but I'm confident it will help."

It was my turn to sigh wearily. I rubbed my face and approached the blind creature.

"Come, let's see how many of your friends are still alive."

"You're going to help us?" He said excitedly.

"Maybe," I said, sounding grumpy.

Chapter Sixteen

THE SIP OF HOPE

We returned through the tunnel and instead of carnage, the mole-men cowered in one corner with my powerful shifters surrounding them, licking their lips.

"Good, I'm glad you didn't rip them apart. Come on, let's go back up where it's cleaner."

"What's going on?" Kai asked, following me.

"We're going to see if we can help these creatures return to their human state."

"Human?" He said, glancing back at the leader. "Were all of them human?"

"Yep, now come." I didn't feel like going into the details at the moment. I wanted to sort this out so that I could go back to my evening in peace.

I traversed back through the tunnels toward the warehouse with my shifters following me, while Eddie led his mole-men behind us. There were twenty-two blind critters, and they desperately needed a shower.

The moment everyone was through the hole and standing around the wooden crate they'd destroyed, I pointed toward the showers. "Clean up while I prepare the Holy Grail for your sipping."

Once my shifters were back in their human form, they helped the mole-men clean while the females prepared something for everyone to eat.

I cleaned the Holy Grail then poured freshly blessed water half-way. I was careful not to mess since holy water scarred vampires and if we drank it we would perish, therefore I would not be testing whether it was pure.

"Is there anything else you need?" Father Neville asked, tugging nervously on his tie. His liver-spotted hand shook, and his tired eyes flittered from the Holy Grail to my face and back again.

I'd asked him not to wear his cassock, but a suit and tie. I wasn't allergic to his black garment, but having a priest inside my warehouse was enough religion I could handle for one day. Him wearing his best suit made the event more informal than sitting through a dreaded Sunday service.

"Take a sip," I said, handing him the Holy Grail.

Father Neville's eyes widened, and he grabbed his chest like his heart was about to give in. He glanced around nervously. "Is that what I think it is?" He asked, staring at the Holy Grail in my hand.

"Yes, now take it before I shove it down your throat," I said, pushing the artifact into his face.

"But—"

"Now, Father." I almost spilled the contents over my hand, forcing myself to take a step backward and relax. "Please, I need to make sure this works." I tapped the side of the chalice with my index fingernail.

"If that is the real thing, that would mean…" He left his words hanging.

"That's right, we don't know what it truly means, but if

you take a sip now and it works, then I can use it on my friends. Maybe it turns them back into humans."

Father Neville hesitantly took the Holy Grail from my hand and brought it near his lips. His piercing brown eyes stared unforgivingly at me. I nodded. He closed his eyes and had a small sip.

Once he'd enjoyed his second sip, he gave the chalice back to me and stepped backward. His chest rose and fell, and sweat peppered his face.

I placed the Holy Grail on the table beside us and reached for him. He waved me away as he fell into the chair behind him. Fanning his face, Father Neville sucked in deep breaths of air, trying desperately to calm down.

One thing I'd learned in all the years I'd been around was never to tell someone to calm down; it was counterproductive.

"How do you feel?" I asked instead.

Father Neville licked his dry lips and swallowed hard. When he found his voice, he finally said, "I don't know."

I neatened my shirt and watched for signs of changes. At first there was nothing, but then...

Noise erupted behind me as the furry creatures exited the bathroom and approached.

My shifters and their mates approached from the other side and offered them food.

When I turned to ask Father Neville if he was hungry, I swallowed my words.

The scar across Father Neville's left temple had disappeared, and the wrinkles next to his eyes and mouth had smoothed out. The salt in his hair became pepper, along with more hair on top.

"I feel wonderful," he said, standing and rubbing his

chest. "And it doesn't feel like my heart is about to beat out of my chest."

"I need you to fill this again when it's empty," — I gave him the chalice, — "now let's see if it changes our furry mole-men back into humans."

Eddie stepped forward first. The now young Father Neville carefully handed him the chalice with a sincere smile and stood to one side.

Eddie glanced blindly toward his mole-friends; their star-noses twitched nervously as they, too, looked in his direction. My shifters stood behind them, waiting anxiously. While I leaned against the far divider, watching everyone. My cellphone vibrated in my pocket; I didn't need to look because I knew it was one of my vampires who needed me. I had things to tend to.

Eddie pressed the chalice against his weird shaped lips and had a sip. He stood motionless, his nose continued twitching. A hiccup passed his lips and then he handed the chalice back to Father Neville.

We stared at him for about five minutes and nothing happened. My frown matched my shifters and even Father Neville seemed confused.

"Okay—" I said. I wanted to say we should try something else when Eddie doubled over and more fur covered his already furry body, making him look like a grizzly-bear-mole. He fell to the ground, knocking his head hard, and continued moaning.

I pushed through the crowd of shifters and whining mole-men, standing closer so that I could see Eddie. When I reached the front, a layer of blisters covered his hairy body and they began bursting. Eddie moaned and groaned as pus oozed out of the blisters, making everyone cringe.

I leaned forward and wrinkled my nose; a foul smell

emitted out of his bubbling sores, forcing everyone to step back in case he exploded. The last thing I needed was gunk all over my suit, but then again, running in sewage water and ripping it in the tunnels had already ruined it.

I sighed wearily and stepped back.

Eddie's hairy skin bubbled and more liquid oozed out of his sores. Steam emitted from his still furry body. Then nothing happened.

The mole-men must've sensed something because they started talking and screeching among themselves. Then silence.

I turned to the front, and the skin on the floor moved, followed by fingers piercing a hole through the hairy barrier. When more fingers pierced the skin and tore a larger hole, the mole-men's noses twitched excitedly.

Finally, a man pushed through the skin and stood naked before us with the widest smile I'd ever seen.

"Hi," human Eddie said. "It works."

Chapter Seventeen

THE LAST ONE

Once the last mole-man sipped from the chalice and left his dirty, hairy skin behind, I ordered the new humans to clean the mess, saving my poor shifters from having to do it.

Father Neville had brought second-hand clothing with him and handed items out to each of the new humans as they hatched from their old skin.

"Léon, wait up." A fully clothed Eddie yelled as he approached with a broad smile. He tucked the wrinkled shirt into his pants and combed his fingers through his disheveled hair. "I just want to thank you for taking a chance on us. I can't fathom what would've happened if you didn't."

"You'd probably stay in the sewers until you all died," I said, not wanting to beat around the bush.

Eddie's smile fell from his face, but he quickly schooled his features and smiled thinly. "Yes, well," — he coughed into his hands, — "anyway, I just wanted to say thank you."

"I won't say it was a pleasure because it wasn't," I said loudly. "And before you all disappear into the night…" I left my words hanging to ensure they all stopped what they were doing and looked at me. "I don't want you to say a word to anyone about what happened here today."

I glanced up from studying Eddie to look at the new humans staring bewildered at me. "I know who each of you are, but I still need you to register with Father Neville with your full names and where you'll be heading. And if you are staying in Sterling Meadow, we can see about finding jobs and housing for you."

I was quiet for a moment, ensuring they were all paying attention before I continued. "Do not tell anyone what happened here today. This artifact cannot get into the wrong hands," — my eyes flitted to Father Neville, who continued fidgeting with his tie, — "don't make me come after you." I warned.

All the heads nodded, and they mumbled words of thanks and promises not to say a word.

"Good. Now, don't forget to register," I said, pointing at Father Neville, who grabbed the pen and paper from Naomi's hands.

The new humans dressed, spoke among themselves, and formed a line to register with the priest. There were odd jobs I could offer some, and I was sure the Were-Animal Alliance could help the rest. My town was big enough to accommodate them all.

One good thing that happened today was that the Holy Grail worked. But should word get out about its benefits, someone daring would try to steal it again, and I couldn't allow that. I needed to hide it somewhere safer and not in my warehouse; perhaps I shouldn't know its whereabouts either.

One person came to mind who could store an artifact and not tell anyone, my Blaire. She was a supernatural assassin who didn't take crap from anyone, including myself and my brother, Sebastian, who was her other lover. I knew she was the perfect person to hide this.

I placed the Holy Grail into a snug cardboard box, into a velvet bag, and then into a backpack.

"Where are you taking it?" Kai asked as he walked with me toward the side exit.

"None of your business." I stopped in the doorjamb and faced Kai. "I need your help to ensure the new humans are safe in Father Neville's hands."

"Yeah, sure," Kai said, glancing over his shoulder at the priest. "Anything else?" He said, looking back at me.

"The girls can stay and they don't have to work, but please, I need my shifters keeping this place safe." I raised the backpack for effect. "There are items you know nothing about, and there's a reason I don't keep a catalogue of all my artifacts. Keep. Everything. Safe."

"Yes, Léon, promise."

"Good, leopard. I must go," I said, stepping out into the midnight moon, then turned back, adding, "One more thing."

"Yes."

"I have a new shipment arriving tomorrow," I said, arching an eyebrow. "Whatever anyone says, don't open it."

Kai swallowed hard and nodded.

I grinned, satisfied with how the day had turned out and that I succeeded in scaring my shifters once more. The parcel arriving tomorrow was only a new couch for their lady friends, but he didn't need to know that now.

Also By N Gray

Blaire Thorne Series

vinci-books.com/ulysses-exposed

I don't know who I am—but my enemies do.

I woke up with no memory, no powers—yet something inside me
is waking up. A vampire saved me. A were-leopard protects me.
But as my past resurfaces, I wonder: am I the hero... or the
monster they fear?

Turn the page for a free preview…

Ulysses Exposed: Chapter One

The air was cool, the sun warm against my face. I was sure it was evening in Sterling Meadow, and not daytime at the beach.

I pushed my fingers into the sand, but the hard concrete beneath shattered my dream. My eyes fluttered open. I was lying on cold ground, looking up at the dark night and the shiny stars scattered beautifully like diamonds across the sky. There were no clouds to ruin my view. It was peaceful and serene.

I glanced to my left, but an ache exploded at the back of my head, my blood trying to thump its way out. My eyes flitted to the sky once again. My pulse thundered in my ears, my eyes clouded over with dark swirls and stars of my own, forcing me to lay still for a breath.

When I lifted my left arm, I couldn't raise it any higher than my body before pain caught me in my ribs. I made a small yelping sound and lowered my arm back to the cold ground.

I raised my right arm, lifting it all the way to my head,

and felt something wet and sticky in my hair. Bringing my hand into view but there was no bright red; only the dark maroon liquid dripping from my fingertips.

I didn't remember much before I saw the stars in the night sky. I didn't remember how I got here, wherever here was.

With effort, I sat up, leaning on my right elbow, but my vision swirled and a headache blossomed. When I could focus again, I scanned my shadowy surroundings. A large dumpster was in front of me, full of garbage. Now that I could see it, I could also smell it. The stench wafted upon the air; the disposal trucks hadn't collected in a while.

Behind the dumpster was a brick wall with boxes on the floor and trash strewn around. It looked like an average alley, except it's not a place that anyone should lay in.

I tried to sit, my breathing now labored, but pain tore through my abdomen and flooded all the way to my toes. A soft cry escaped my mouth. Beads of sweat trickled down my face as I pushed with both arms until I was leaning against the wall. In a half-sitting, half-lying position, I slowly bent my knees and noticed that my jeans were ripped, a wound on my left thigh visibly oozing a dark, murky liquid.

It looked like claw marks. The only animal large enough to inflict a serious injury like this was a were-animal.

Were-animals had been living among humans for a while now; along with all the other monsters, vampires, witches, warlocks, fairies and dragons, to name just a few. We, the humans, tried not to be food for any of them, and there were laws protecting us against the monsters.

Being attacked by any were-animal, if it didn't kill me, could leave me infected with the viral strain or virus of that specific were-animal.

Shit!

If I survived—which was a big '*if*'—I would turn furry once a month when the moon was full. I didn't want *that* to happen. Nobody did.

I wiped sweat from my forehead and pulled the rest of my shirt out from the waistband of my jeans, looking to see why there was so much pain in my side. I wore a black vest beneath a black blouse, and the two pieces of clothing came out of my jeans easily as I pulled. Pain cut through my side again and I clenched my jaw. I lifted the two shirts higher, exposing my black bra, but as I was the only one there, there was no embarrassment necessary.

I froze when I saw an empty shoulder holster, a gun nowhere in sight. I hoped I had a license for the gun— humans got jail time for carrying a weapon without that piece of paper.

With both shirts pulled high, I saw the wound. There were small chunks of flesh missing from my left-hand side; the soft delicate meat between my hip bone and ribs was gone, chewed and swallowed by something with big teeth. The wound had tears splitting from it that almost reached my belly button, like the were-animal had wanted to rip me apart.

As I pressed gently on the wound, blood gushed thick and heavy from beneath my fingers, and the night sky swirled before me again.

When I came to a few seconds later, the wound was still trickling blood. If an organ had been nicked by the animal's teeth, there might not be enough time. If I was going to survive, I needed to do something quick.

I unbuttoned my blouse and steadily slipped it off my shoulders. With my teeth and hands, I tore the blouse in half, scrunched one half into a tight ball, and pressed it gently against the wound on my side. Tears began to trickle down my cheeks and onto my chest. I pulled the vest down to cover the wound and to hold the make-shift gauze in place. With the other half of the blouse, I flattened it out and twisted it so that it looked like a long rope and tied it around my thigh. It was the best I could do to stop the bleeding without having a belt.

With the tourniquet in place, a sharp, shooting pain vibrated up my spine and down to my toes as I secured the knot on my thigh, allowing me the freedom to hold the wound on my side closed with both hands.

I felt all the pain; the tearing of the bite wound and the pulling of the clawed wound as the adrenaline tapered off. I lay quietly, concentrating on my breathing and contemplating my next move.

I could scream for help and try to crawl out from the alley. But, there was a problem with that. I didn't think I would be able to move with this hole in my side, and I didn't know the neighborhood. There could be monsters leering around every corner, hungry to taste fresh human meat, and the moment they saw me they'd pounce. Vampires loved blood. Were-animals loved flesh. Witches could use me for their spells.

Shit.

My pulse hammered in my ears, and tiny sparks fluttered in my vision. I needed help. Now!

I sat straighter against the wall, my body positioned slightly to the right so that the wound on my left wasn't compromised. As I bent forward, something thicker than tears ran down my face. I'd been so concerned about the wounds on my leg and abdomen that I'd forgotten about the wound on my head. I wiped it away with the back of my hand to find more of the dark, thick liquid. This had to be the worst evening ever.

My breath caught in my throat when the sounds of men talking and footsteps nearing. They were almost at the opening of the alley. There was maybe three or four of them. I didn't know if they were good men and would help, or whether they would finish the job the were-animal had started. If they were vampires and saw all this blood, then I was the perfect victim. I hadn't heard of a vampire that could resist so much blood. And no were-animal could resist biting into fresh flesh. I was a *Happy Meal* to go.

But, I needed help urgently. I had to risk being discovered or I'd die a very slow, and painful death.

At first, I cried out softly. When they didn't respond, I cried out louder. The talking stopped, and the footsteps slowed down. I glanced over my right shoulder to see the entrance of the alley and rested my head; it was too much effort to keep my head up. In the light, I saw three of them, one slightly ahead of the others. They were staring at me.

Their eyes glowed like a cat's would when in the dark. The men were were-animals, and I was potentially vulnerable prey. The man in front, his face concealed in darkness, stood painfully still; possibly tempted at the dying woman on the ground.

I cried out again, this time a whimper, as the pain ripped through my body.

The men spoke quietly to each other, then the man in front nodded.

I closed my eyes for a second and when I opened them again, two men entered the alley and headed toward me. When they reached me, one crouched down and showed me his hands, letting me know he had no weapons and meant no harm. I hoped.

I tried to speak, but no sound came out. I cleared my throat and tried again. "Help me," I whispered.

"Your leg is bleeding. I will try to stop it and then pick you up. If we don't help you now, you will die here." He looked up at his friend and then back at me. "Can you hear me?"

"Yes." I nodded and swallowed hard. I think everyone around the block heard me swallow. "Please help me."

"Give me your belt," the man said to his friend, lifting his hand to wait for the belt. When he had it in his hands, he wrapped it around my left thigh and fastened tightly to stop the bleeding. When he pulled on it, to fasten the belt into place, I cried out until the night swallowed me.

Ulysses Exposed: Chapter Two

I woke in a stranger's arms. He carried me like a sleeping child with my right arm draped loosely around his neck. I tensed and grabbed hold of his neck as if I would fall.

He must have felt me move because he patted me gently on my arm.

"It's okay. I've got you. I won't let you fall," he said, gazing down at me. "I'm Sebastian. What's your name?"

"Ah," I started to say, then furrowed my brows. "I don't remember."

I didn't know my name. It was stuck, right there but just out of reach. A headache thumped at my temples, and the streetlights above us swam in swirls as I swallowed hard. I closed my eyes and thought about the sky, the fresh Chinese take-away smell wafting in the air, and the ocean—we were nowhere near the ocean, but I smelled it, nevertheless. I swallowed again, chasing down the vomit—throwing up would not be a good idea, not with my pulse thudding behind my eyes.

"We need to take her to casualty." This from Sebastian's friend, who was walking beside him.

"She needs help urgently," Sebastian said. "She won't make the trip."

"If we drop her off at the medical center, they will not treat her. They aren't equipped to handle her condition properly." This was the first time the man who walked ahead had spoken.

I opened my eyes, but all I saw was his dark brown hair brushed close to his head and stayed in place as he glided onward. And he wore a beautiful luxury coat that flowed to his ankles and billowed behind him in mystery and intrigue.

Sebastian did his best to walk without hurting me, but every now and again pain shot up my left leg and dug deeply into my side. All the while, the headache burned through my brain. My blood was on fire as it moved through my veins, and I winced with each step Sebastian took. I didn't know if I could manage going any farther.

I cried out and grabbed my left-hand side. Flesh started tearing near my bellybutton and spine like I was being torn in two. I wondered whether my insides would exit the wound.

I didn't know what it was about this attack, but this didn't feel normal. Nothing about an attack was normal, but this, this was something else; the burning of my skin, the fire in my blood and the feel of my flesh as it kept tearing.

None of it was *normal*.

Sebastian moved me slightly in his arms so that he could gently lay his hand over mine as I held onto my side.

"We are almost at my master's place," he said gently. "Just one more block." He smiled, but there was sadness in his eyes.

I didn't know this kind man helping me and couldn't

interpret his expressions but the tenderness of his touch, as comforting as it was, left me worried. Whatever had happened to me in that alley might be the death of me.

But if I was about to die, I needed something to take my mind off death, and tear my thoughts away from the pain.

I glanced up at Sebastian; I might as well admire the view. He was beautiful; his lips full and kissable, grass green eyes with slivers of gold running through them and long eyelashes. He had high cheekbones, a square jaw, and the ear that I could see was nicely shaped and sat neatly against his head. He had short blonde hair that was shaved at the sides and a little longer on top, so that you could just see the beginning of velvety curls. His hair so soft I wanted to run my fingers through it. But there was something else about him.

"Which animal are you?" I asked, barely audible; my speech came as more of a mumble.

This wasn't the best time to make idle chit-chat, but I desperately wanted to stop thinking about the pain while my blood ran hot. The only thing I could think of was to talk.

"I'm a were-leopard." He flashed a wholesome grin. "How did you know?"

I didn't answer him. My eyes were heavy, and I rested my head on his broad shoulders, but I think I smiled. I couldn't remember.

And then I died.

Okay, I didn't die. I passed out from all the blood loss. I awoke to bright lights above me, and someone tugging on my abdomen. My whole body shook as they pulled down. I tried to sit, but small hands came from behind the little curtain in front of me and pushed me back onto the table.

"Don't sit. I'm busy suturing your side." Big brown eyes commanded from behind a pair of glasses, and her mouth was hidden behind a mask.

"Léon, I need help. It's too much; it's too deep."

The doctor stopped pulling on me and turned around. I looked to the left to see who she was talking to, and it was the other man—the one who had walked in front. His name was Léon. That name rang familiar. I knew it from somewhere. Just like my name, it's sitting on the tip of my tongue, but I couldn't say it.

One moment Léon was across the room, the next he stood beside the doctor—so close I could lift my hand and touch him. Either he had used magic, or I was just slow; it could've been both. I did a slow blink trying to process this information and stared at him.

He was talking to the doctor, but he stared at me. I saw his mouth move but couldn't comprehend what he was saying. He had exquisite eyes; they were ocean blue. Eyes you could look at every day. The blue of water so deep that you could fall into and drown. The dark brown or black hair framed a pale face with high cheekbones and a strong jaw.

They were whispering under their breath. I didn't know why I wanted to do this, it's like you always want to do the thing you shouldn't because it's not a good idea, but it's what I did. I tried to move my right arm, but it was heavy. I lifted it and a block of wood came with it along with the drip. Someone came into my view from above and grabbed my arm to move it back into place.

"Don't move," he whispered near the shell of my ear as

he moved hair out of my face. "Relax, we will take care of you."

I couldn't see who it was, but his voice was smooth and soothing as velvet, and I relaxed my arm in his.

"Give her another shot."

I noticed the doctor watching me, as was Léon. Both their faces were blank, devoid of any emotion or telltale signs of what they were really thinking.

Someone had their back to me and was tinkering with the drip. Another slow blink, and I closed my eyes.

Hard grinding sounds and heavy moving concrete stirred me awake. I did not understand what the sound was, but it felt like the earth or I were moving. My arm rested around someone's waist, and they were gently cupping my hand in theirs. Their skin was warm and smelled of the ocean, with just a hint of citrus. There was also the smell of leaves and grass mixed in somewhere. I snuggled my face against their back, and it felt so warm, so safe.

What did I do last night to wake in someone's bed? I tensed. Opening my eyes, I wanted to take my hand away, but he held onto my hand and started turning around to face me. I kept tugging on my arm to set it free, but he kept holding on as he turned around. My chest tightened as I held my breath. As he faced me, I recognized him. It was Sebastian, the man who had carried me. He smiled, and we were close enough that I could see how green his eyes were, even with the slivers of gold—they reminded me of eyes on black kitty cats, the color of true green without the gray hues that most green-eyed people had.

His intense stare made me avert my eyes to see if I was

wearing anything. The sheet came up under my arms. It covered everything, but I peeked inside the covers to see if I was naked—which I was, except for underwear. Thank goodness I still had *something* on.

Why was he in bed with me? I hoped he wasn't naked. The sheet was tucked underneath him from turning around, so that all I could see was his naked chest and waist. I felt heat creep up my neck. His smile widened. I pulled the sheet higher and tucked it all around me.

"Why are you in bed with me—and please tell me you are not naked?"

"Don't worry, your virtue is safe." He chuckled. "We have great healing capabilities, not only for were-animals but for humans as well. We took turns lying with you."

Someone moved behind me, and a squeal sound escaped my lips.

She laughed and said, "I don't like women, sweetheart." She patted me on my shoulder. "How do you feel?" She sat up far enough so that I could see her face. She too wore underwear—a navy sports bra with black panties. She threw the covers off and climbed out the bed.

"I don't know how I feel. I don't feel any pain, I think." I frowned.

I laid flat on my back and made sure the duvet tucked in everywhere. I straightened my legs and flexed my toes; something tightened around my left thigh, and a small cry escaped my mouth. Stitches pulled when I stretched my legs. My arms were above the covers, and I felt my left-hand side. There was something covering the wound—I'd look when I was alone. I didn't want to lift the covers and flash anyone. I might have flashed when they put me in the bed, but as I wasn't awake, that didn't count.

I lifted my hand to my head and felt stitches above my

left eye, and more stitches on the side of my head where a section of my hair had been shaved. I could hide the wound when my hair was loose. I was lucky to be alive.

I watched the woman pull on jeans and a black t-shirt. She added a shoulder holster and put her gun in place. I tensed when she caught my eye.

"We are guards for the master." She answered my question without having to be asked, and she patted her gun like it was a pet.

"Which animal are you?" I said, my eyes flitting from her gun to her face.

She sat on the edge of the bed and pulled on socks and shoes. "I'm a were-rat, and he's a were-leopard." She pointed to Sebastian.

Okay, now I remembered Sebastian telling me he was a were-leopard when he carried me.

"Can you remember anything?" Sebastian asked.

I faced him. Sebastian had moved and sat against the headboard.

"No," I said, shaking my head at the same time—it didn't hurt. Yay for me! "How long have I been here?"

"Two days."

"Shit. Has it been *two days*? They ripped me to shreds, and I almost died. How come I feel so good? I shouldn't be feeling *this* good, should I?"

"Like I said, we are good at healing." Sebastian's smile reached his stunning green eyes, the color of fresh green leaves after a summer's rain.

"I don't suppose you know which were-animal attacked me and whether I will change into something furry at the next full moon?"

The two guards shared a look, but Sebastian answered. "We don't know. The doctor will take blood in a day or two for testing, and we will see at the end of the month if there are any," — he hesitated, perhaps trying to find the right word, — "*changes*."

"Do you know if anyone has been looking for me? I should probably go to the police."

"Well, sweetheart," the were-rat stood and combed her fingers through her short brown hair, styled in a bob. "I think the police already have enough cases, and your file might fall to the bottom of their shit-list. Don't take this personally, but you might have to figure this one out on your own."

She must have seen the shock on my face and added, "I'm Elena." She smiled. To Sebastian she said, "Hang back and give her the in's and out's of everything; I'm sure they will fetch her for dinner later, or you can take her there yourself if you aren't busy." She waved goodbye and left.

Sebastian moved beside me and pulled the sheet off completely, revealing low hanging boxers. He had broad shoulders and a slim waist beneath a well-developed inguinal crease. He caught me staring, and I felt heat rise up my neck and face. He grinned mischievously and grabbed his clothing from a table.

I frowned with a hint of anger just below the surface; I guessed it's easier to be angry than embarrassed.

As if he knew I was still watching, Sebastian pulled his black jeans and t-shirt on seductively, and slow enough so that I could see all his muscles move. I licked dry lips. He wore a similar uniform to Elena.

Sebastian went to a shelf on the far wall and came back with a heap of clothing and toiletries which he placed on the bed near to me.

"We had to cut your old clothing from your body. Fortunately, the master arranged for new clothes for you. The bathroom is there," — he pointed to a door on his left, — "the doctor said you can shower with the plasters on." I nodded, feeling the dirt caked on my body, I needed a shower desperately. "I'll wait for you to freshen up so take your time, and then I'll take you to the kitchen for something to eat."

"Thank you," I said, pulling the sheet out from where it was tucked under the mattress and bunched it around my body like a large fluffy dress. Climbing off the bed was difficult with the sheet, but I tried to be as ladylike as I could whilst grabbing the pile of items with my free hand.

"Thank you for helping me back there in the alley. And for carrying me, and now for this; for healing me."

"It was nothing."

"Really? You save me, and it's nothing?"

"Why not?" His face was pleasant. There was no malice hidden there, only an honest face, clean shaven and almost innocent-looking. "We helped you because we could."

We held eye contact for a few seconds, and then I asked, "Who is this master you two keep referring to?"

"Léon. Does his name ring a bell?"

I shook my head. "Only from two nights ago, when you found me. But I don't really remember."

"He is the master of all the were-animals and vampires in Sterling Meadow."

I shrugged. The attack had taken the memory of who I was and everything else I knew before two days ago. I remembered Sterling Meadow, how to walk and talk. I knew which day it was but I didn't know who I was and I didn't know Léon.

The thought of not knowing left me frustrated. I was a shell of my former self, desperately needing to piece the puzzle of my life back together again.

If the police weren't able to help, would Léon or Sebastian? They didn't know me, and they didn't owe me anything, so why should they help me? I already owed them my life.

Now that Léon had gone out of his way to help me, I didn't know if he wanted something in return. Did I owe him a favor now? If I did, what would that favor entail? Vampires schemed and plotted and used their power against each other. Their eyes alone could control humans. I didn't know what I'd do if Léon wanted to control *me*.

I was standing with the sheet around my body and clutching the items in my hands. Fatigue enveloped me and all I wanted to do was clean up before I became lethargic. "Okay," I said, my throat dry. "Let me shower quickly so we can eat," I said when my stomach grumbled.

I locked the bathroom door and placed the clothing and toiletries beside the neatly rolled white towels on the white marble table near the bath. The tiles all around, cream with dark swirls on them, made the walls come alive as you walked into the bathroom. The basin, toilet, and bath were black—a stark contrast to the usual white or cream. The shower could fit at least six people with enough jets to massage all your aching muscles at the same time, and the bath could seat at least four adults comfortably. The bathroom was huge and dark, but the colors blended well.

One wall was entirely dominated by mirrored glass, so that whatever you did in the shower or bath was in full view of anyone you shared the room with. I glanced at the mirror. I didn't want to see the damage, but I had to look.

I faced the mirror and dropped the sheet. I stared at my body. The three deep lines running across my left thigh had been stitched neatly. It must've been a large claw of a werepredator to cause that kind of damage.

I touched my abdomen lightly. I felt all the stitches through the large plaster that covered from my bellybutton all the way around to near my spine. Still trailing lightly along the edge of the plaster, near my pelvis, was a scar running up my abdomen. It was a low vertical caesarian section scar that was old and didn't hurt when I ran my fingers over it. Doctors didn't take procedures like that lightly; the baby I'd carried had to come out immediately.

With everything that had happened, I hadn't thought of anything else. There was a possibility that, somewhere, I had a child waiting for me, and that I was married or lived with someone.

Something tightened in my chest. There could be someone waiting for me to come home. They might *need* me to come home.

Shit.

I twisted my body around so that I could see the full length of the large plaster and saw a tattoo of a butterfly—a Ulysses butterfly. Not a small dainty one on a shoulder, but a large 3D version with a wingspan of at least four inches on each shoulder blade. It was beautiful. It looked as though the butterfly could take flight from my back. The wings were shaded with bright blues and greens, and as I neared the mirror to see the detail, I saw each wing had been finely tattooed with intricate details that must have taken days to complete. The outline of the wings looked like hieroglyphic symbols, so small that the artist must have used the smallest needle possible, which came with a lot of pain.

It was hard to believe that this was who I was, a tattooed mother running around the streets at night. Alone.

I combed my fingers through my hair until I found the shaved section. It didn't hurt; surely, I should feel some pain? The stitches felt spiky against my fingertips as they brushed the smooth, naked skin surrounding it. My green eyes dark and were very close to a gray or charcoal color. My left eye socket and cheek were bruised, and already changing color like blossoming flowers in spring. The stitches above my eye were finer, and their immaculate presentation suggested that they might not leave a scar at all.

I should be dead with this amount of injury. I was not a were-animal or a vampire, and I didn't have any mystical powers. It was impossible that I had survived, and yet I had.

The confusion I felt was more than I could bear. I must've hit my head pretty hard not to be able to remember anything, and I needed to understand why I was alone in that alley.

A headache started, and I didn't want to think anymore.

With great care, I removed the underwear that I had awoken wearing, unsuccessfully trying to avoid any stabs of pain from my wounds. As I stood there naked in the unfamiliar bathroom, the true nature of the ordeal that I had sustained tore through me.

I climbed into the hot shower and cried. I let the tears flow down my face and mix with the hot water. I stood where no-one could hear or see me, and I held myself. I shivered under the hot water as it fell on my skin, and it felt good; I felt alive.

When I was ready to wash, I glanced at all the expensive-looking bottles standing on the glass shelves against the wall in the shower. The shampoo was French, as was the conditioner, and I used both to wash the traces of red from my long brown hair. As the water ran through it, my hair felt smooth and smelled fresh, vaguely reminding me of the scent of the ocean. The delicate and clean soap, also from France, had hints of citrus, lavender, and plum. I washed

N GRAY

my body with the soap, and the foam cleaned all the dried blood away from my aching body.

My muscles didn't ache as much when I climbed out of the shower. It was only the sharp pull of the stitches in my skin that burned when I moved.

As drops of water ran along the contours of my body, I began to dry myself with one of the large towels from the table, wrapping it around my body so that it hung all the way to my shins.

Once dry, I took the toiletries from the table and set them near the basin. I brushed my teeth, applied some deodorant and used the face cream that was standing near the mirror beside the other little bottles. I rolled my eyes. I couldn't help but notice that *all* the cosmetics were French. I guessed that it was true what people said about vampires; some were unnecessarily elegant.

I reached for the fresh clothing that I had left beside the bath. The bra was lace and matched the panties, both silky and expensive. The underwear I had previously worn was all cotton and didn't match. As I slipped them on, I realized that, apart from the fact that they fitted perfectly, they were strangely comfortable. The new jeans were a perfect fit to the curve of my hips and slender waist. The black v-neck t-shirt was just as comfortable, and luckily the lace bra I wore beneath wasn't push-up, so there was no cleavage showing.

I stared at my toned body in the new outfit and flexed my bicep muscles. As soon as I had, I smiled. I looked like one of the guards in my black shirt and jeans.

I opened the bathroom door and saw Sebastian sitting in the chair reading a book. He glanced at me and frowned.

"What?"

"Your hair," he chortled.

"Shit." As soon as he mentioned it, I realized that my

unkempt hair was still sodden from the shower. I went back into the bathroom, bent my body forward and towel-dried it.

When I came up, Sebastian stood next to me, holding a spray bottle.

"Turn around."

I warily did as he asked, staring at him in the mirror as he sprayed the stuff onto my hair.

"It will keep your hair soft."

I picked up a comb, and it glided through my hair like a hot knife through butter. My hair began to straighten, and, as Sebastian had promised, it *was* soft.

"Is this your room?" I asked him

"No, it's the master's."

"Shit."

"You say 'shit' a lot." He grinned.

"Well, yeah. You might, too, if you were me. I feel like I have invaded the man's personal space, and now I've used all his products."

"Don't worry about it. The master is a very generous host. You're welcome to use anything you find." In the mirror's reflection, Sebastian smiled, and although the warmth there seemed genuine, I also saw glimpses of darkness behind the alluring green eyes. He held my gaze for a moment before he spoke again, turning for the door. "Come, let's go eat."

I followed Sebastian out.

Grab your copy...
vinci-books.com/ulysses-exposed

About the Author

A Multi-genre author writing twisted endings...

N Gray is a USA Today Bestselling Author who lives in Cape Town, South Africa, with her daughter and adopted cat named Miss Beans.

During the day, she's an analyst and provider profiler for a medical insurance company. At night, she types on her curved keyboard, creating fictional characters some may love and others you want to kill yourself.

She writes in four genres: urban fantasy, thriller, horror, and paranormal romance.

She now writes under Natalie Michaels for her new thrillers and SD Syns for her new horrors.

Acknowledgments

Thank you to my readers, old and new, for taking a chance on my books.

You are the reason I write the stories I do. As long as you keep reading, I'll keep writing.

I'm truly humbled by your support and encouragement.

I write in as many genres as I love reading in. There are so many stories swarming inside my head that I could never just choose one.

Horror is my guilty pleasure. I love writing short stories filled with dark humour and the occult, with a twist ending.

Urban fantasy and paranormal romance are where I love to spend my time, and I have so many books planned that I don't have enough time *(but I'll get there)*.

And lastly, my thrillers. Who doesn't love sitting on the edge of their seat while reading about what goes on inside the antagonist's mind? Well, I love writing about them.